I0679568

MARIE-HÉLÈNE LEBEAULT

THE WORLD JUMPER

THE EVERS SERIES BOOK FOUR

First published by Beaches and Trails Publishing 2020
Copyright © 2020 by Marie-Hélène Lebeault
All rights reserved.

No part of this publication may be reproduced, stored, or transmitted in any form or by
any means, electronic, mechanical, photocopying, recording, scanning, or otherwise
without written permission from the publisher. It is illegal to copy this book, post it to a
website, or distribute it by any other means without permission.
This is a work of fiction.

2025 Edition

Editing by Jacki Corn-Uys
Cover by Getfast

PROLOGUE

WILLIAMSBURG, VA, January 12, 1700

The maid hovered in the doorway, anxiously wringing her hands. She needed to see to her mistress. Lady Evers had passed nigh on sixty minutes, and it was unseemly to make her spirit wait to cross over.

But Sir Evers still knelt by his wife's bedside, clutching her hand, weeping softly as he implored his beloved to come back to him.

The midwife had urged him to leave her side so the women could attend to her, entreating him to come and meet his son and daughter, both hale and hearty. Lord Evers became agitated and bellowed, "Find a witch. Surely one of them can revive her!"

The midwife had shaken her head, placed a hand on his arm, and replied, "Sir, the witches have all been executed, but even they would tell you there is no coming back from the dead."

In the end, she left after making arrangements for a wet nurse to care for the babies. Though she was not a witch herself, she suspected Lady Evers had been one, as was Annie, her lady's maid. On her way out, she had taken Annie aside.

"You'll be wanting to bind the children's magic as soon as possible. Though the witch hunts are over, I don't need to tell you that your kind will never be safe."

Annie had feigned ignorance, but there was no fooling the old midwife. She nodded and closed the door behind the woman.

Annie was not as skilled nor as knowledgeable as her employer, but it was clear she needed to act swiftly before anyone else arrived. It was lucky that Lady Evers had given birth in the middle of the night. Apart from Sir Evers, the midwife, and herself, the only other person aware of the birth was a footman who'd been roused to fetch the midwife. After being asked to carry hot water and other items from the kitchen, he was dismissed and promptly returned to bed.

Sir Evers still wept and Annie turned. If she could not attend to Lady Evers, she could at least do as the midwife implored. The babies must be protected.

The children were in matching baskets by the fire in the parlor. Annie gathered what she needed for the binding spell: a candle, some string, and a pair of poppets. She made quick work of it. It was an easy spell to do. Later, when there was more time, she would also perform a protection spell and prepare amulets for the children. But for the time being, they were safe here at home. She gently touched both of their soft cheeks before returning to Lady Evers' room.

As she gazed at the mourning Lord, she squared her shoulders and strode into the room with more confidence than she felt. She grabbed a firm hold of the man's arm and tugged gently.

"Sir, I really must insist you let me attend to my lady. Her spirit hovers and wants to be set free," she implored.

Archibald, upon hearing about his wife's spirit, looked up and faced the maid. She nodded and nudged his arm away from the bed.

"Your children are in the parlor. The wet nurse should arrive at any moment now. I'll be as quick as I can," she assured him.

The man finally got up and placed a tender kiss on his wife's forehead. He then kissed the hand he was still clutching and promised to return soon. He headed out of the room but paused in the doorway to look at his wife. The midwife had washed her face, smoothed her hair, and covered her body with the bedclothes. She looked like she was sleeping and could wake at any moment. He took a step toward her, but the maid blocked his way, grim-faced.

"Sir, please," she entreated.

With a choked sob, Archibald turned and left his wife's bed-chamber.

As he entered the parlor, Sir Evers saw the baskets near the fire. Thinking he needed fortification before he met his progeny, he headed for the liquor cabinet. Drink in hand, he walked back to his children and crouched low to get a better view of them. The boy, wrapped in a blue blanket, was sleeping peacefully. His head was covered with a bonnet; there was no way of seeing if he had any hair. It was clear, however, that he favored his mother. He had her round face and delicate nose. He looked over at the boy's sister and was surprised to see her eyes were open. She seemed to be staring directly at him. He leaned in closer and smiled. She had somehow managed to free her hands from the yellow blanket. He reached in and lifted the tiny hand with his finger. His daughter's hand closed around it firmly. It was all it took for Archibald to lose his heart to yet another Evers sorceress.

The spell was broken when he heard a sound in the hall. Thinking it must be Annie coming to fetch him to take him back to his wife's room, he rose and let his finger slip out of his daughter's grasp.

She was having none of it and immediately started wailing. In a panic, he tried to coo at her, to no avail. It seemed to incense her more than anything, and soon she'd woken her brother.

"Annie!" he bellowed.

Where was the blasted girl when you needed her? he thought.

And then he remembered, and grief reached into his heart and squeezed. He knelt on the floor and placed a hand on each of his children's bellies, hoping to soothe them as he rubbed gently. It seemed to calm them. He heard shuffling at the door and turned, thinking Annie had finally come to his aid, but there was a man at the door. Though it was winter, the man had neither coat nor hat.

Archibald rose and waited for the butler or a footman to appear and announce the visitor, but the stranger was indeed alone. He didn't look menacing. In fact, he looked like a scholar with his wire-rimmed glasses and his odd attire. There was something very familiar about him.

Nonetheless, he thought it best to put himself between the stranger and his newborns. Archibald strode to him and bowed, "Archibald Evers, at your service."

When the man did not immediately respond, he added, "I apologize for my attire, sir, but, as you may have surmised, it is the middle of the night, and I was not expecting visitors."

The man found his voice and rushed out an apology of his own. "I'm terribly sorry. I've been Traveling and had not realized the time," said the man. "Are those your children?" he asked as he took a step closer to the baskets.

Archibald made a side step to halt his advance. "Perhaps you'd care to tell me what brings you to my home in the middle of the night," said Archibald, a distinct frost in his tone.

"Of course," replied the man. He took a step back and raked his fingers through his hair. "I'm afraid you might not believe me, though."

Archibald raised an eyebrow. "Perhaps you would be so kind as to provide your name, sir," he said and waited for the man to explain himself.

"My name is Simon Evers, and I'm one of your descendants," said the man.

When Lord Evers said nothing, he continued, "I've come from the year 2004." He took out the pocket watch and held it out to Archibald, whose eyes had grown wide at the sight of it.

"Where did you find that?" he asked, reaching for it.

Simon let him have it. Archibald stared at the device in utter bewilderment.

Their conversation was interrupted as Annie knocked on the door, casting a worried look towards the stranger.

"Sir, the wet nurse is here. May we take the children up to the nursery?" she asked, hovering by the door.

He waved her in and saw the wet nurse was just behind her. She curtsied as she entered, first to Archibald, then to his guest. Archibald asked what her name was. "Elizabeth, sir, but everyone calls me Lizzie," was her reply.

"Thank you for coming, Lizzie. I assume Annie has told you about the children's mother?" he asked.

"Yes, sir. I'm ever so sorry for your loss," she said, bowing her head in respect and crossing herself. "May she rest in peace."

He nodded at her, then at the babies. Annie and Lizzie each took one of the baskets and quickly left the parlor.

Simon looked horrified. He kept opening his mouth to say something, but words were not forthcoming. Finally, Simon cleared his throat and said, "Sir, my sincerest condolences. I had not realized. I should take my leave."

Archibald cut him off. "No, please stay. It's a much-needed distraction. My wife died in childbirth only an hour ago, and I'm afraid I'm not quite ready to deal with that piece of reality. I would much prefer to discuss this bit of fiction instead," he said, indicating the pocket watch in his hand.

"Follow me," he said and led the way out of the parlor, down the hall, and into the study. It looked the same as it did in 2004, except the furniture looked brand new.

Archibald walked over to the desk and opened one of the small, locked cubby drawers. It was empty. He had secured the pocket watch in the drawer only last week. He shot an accusatory look at Simon.

"That's not where I found it," said Simon, who went to one of the floor-to-ceiling bookcases, his fingers feeling the underside of the wood paneling. Finding the spot he was looking for, he pressed it, and a hidden compartment popped out. It was empty.

Archibald got up from the desk and came to look at the compartment. "How did you know that was there?" he asked, amazed. "And for that matter, how did the timepiece get there?"

"It's a long story..." replied Simon.

"Incredible," replied Archibald, nodding. "Are there others?"

Simon went around the room and opened another five hidden compartments. Two of them had items in them. The first was a velour pouch with an assortment of gems. The gems looked genuine, and the pouch was heavy. Archibald pocketed the pouch and looked at the other compartment. This one contained the deeds to multiple parcels of land in the area. It seemed the late Lord Evers had a few tricks up his sleeve. Archibald put the deeds back into the drawer. He had no immediate need for them, but perhaps they would prove useful in the future.

He turned to Simon and gestured to one of the armchairs. Simon accepted the glass that Archibald placed in front of him. Simon raised his glass and said, "To Lady Emmeline, may she rest in peace."

Archibald nodded in acknowledgment and clinked his glass. The men drank their bourbon and talked until morning.

CHAPTER I

JACKSON

WHEN LOLA CAME BACK from The Academy with Devlin in tow, Jackson was immediately suspicious of the new family member. However, after doing his digging, he agreed with the attorney; Devlin seemed legit.

But from then on, everyone started acting like he was superfluous. Of course, they made it look like they were giving him back his freedom and letting him spread his wings. But it hurt being excluded from the only family he had ever known.

When Phyllis had told him about Lola, he hadn't taken it well. He hadn't let it show, of course. Phyllis had been so excited at the prospect of having her long-lost niece stay with her. Phyllis was such a wonderful person, and Jackson loved her like she was his aunt. But she wasn't. She was Lola's aunt. And though he'd been treated as one of the family since he was a child, the truth was that he was the caretakers' child. At best, he was a charity case. At worst, he was the help.

And now that Devlin was there, they didn't need him. Now he felt stupid for delaying college for so long. Sure, Phyllis had pre-paid his tuition, and he had money set aside. But he was two years behind. Bonnie and the others would be graduating this year, and he hadn't even started college. He wasn't even sure he still wanted to study Business at UVA now that he would no longer be the Evers' Estate Manager.

Depressed and confused, he had reached out to Bonnie at Patty's party. She suggested he join her for a weekend at the beach, clear his head, and get some perspective.

"Look, I get that you feel excluded," she said, turning over onto her stomach as they were sunbathing. "But it's not like Phyllis has kicked you out. Take a vacation, see the world, have fun!"

When he started to object, she added, "You're only nineteen! College will be there when you get back. And, honestly, your life sucks. I mean, you have more responsibilities than my parents. You need to lighten up!"

Jackson pondered this for a while. He liked his life. True, most of his friends were either boozing it up in college or working easy jobs to make money for their next adventure. He was lucky to have such a great home, a position he loved and was good at, and plenty of money. Of course, he should take this trip. Enjoy what was left of his youth.

"You're right. My big problem is not that I'm behind in college; it's that I'm behind on my quota of questionable decisions and stupid shenanigans," he told Bonnie as he grabbed a beer from the cooler, popped the can, and chugged the whole thing. Bonnie started hooting and got herself a beer, though she only took a few sips in solidarity. They spent the rest of the weekend wasting time with the locals, overeating at beach cookouts, and dancing the nights away at beach bonfire parties.

When Jackson had gotten home late Sunday night, he relaxed and looked forward to starting a whole new life.

On Monday morning, Jackson met with Phyllis and the new caretakers, John and Sally. They would spend the week training with Jackson and Marie and move in the following weekend if all went well.

Jackson liked John, but he was uneasy about giving him access to all the security protocols. Mr. Radcliff said he and Sally had been cleared and could be trusted with all of the Evers' secrets. But how much did Mr. Radcliff know about what Jackson knew?

After touring the Estate with John, Jackson set him to work in the garage. The cars were due for their monthly cleaning and top-ups. That would keep him busy for a few hours.

Jackson went to his office in the apartment over the garage. That's where the command center was set up. It would need to be moved either to the caretakers' cottage or to the main house study. But for now, it was Jackson's to control.

Devlin, Lola, and Phyllis had been spending a lot of time behind closed doors lately. At first, he figured they just wanted to have some privacy to discuss family matters. But now, he got the feeling something was up. They were unaware that the Estate's security and surveillance equipment was not limited to the grounds.

All the rooms except the bathrooms had cameras. The bedroom cameras didn't record a continuous video feed as that would have been intrusive. However, the feed was live. One of his screens showed a revolving view of the bedrooms, two at a time, and the computer snapped a still picture randomly once every hour. None of the video feeds had sound.

Jackson went over the outdoor feeds recorded since he had left on Friday. Everything seemed in order. He then looked at the indoor feeds, saving the bedrooms for last. Things were quiet until the family came back from the House party. Jackson watched the feed at super speed until something caught his interest. Phyllis, Lola, and Devlin were in the Library having what looked like a heated discussion. Their logbook was on the desk, along with the Pocket Watch and the Marble. From last week's feeds, Jackson knew these were new additions to the family secrets. No one had discussed them with him, and he hadn't seen any of them overtly Traveling either. He couldn't shake the feeling that something terrible was about to happen.

There was a knock at the door, so Jackson pulled up the feed from the garage. John was hard at work, waxing Simon's Maserati. *Maybe it's Lola*, he thought, getting up to answer the door.

But when he opened the door, it wasn't Lola. It was Simon!

"What are you doing here?" hissed Jackson as he pulled Simon into his apartment and quickly closed the door. "Did John see you?"

Simon chuckled as he peered at John on the screen. The new caretaker was enjoying the task at hand.

"Well, hello to you, too!" exclaimed Simon. "I see you are hard at work spying on my family," he added with a wry smile.

Jackson's brows knitted closer as he mentally flipped through several responses to this.

"I'm kidding, Jackson," said Simon as he clapped a hand on the young man's shoulder. "Relax, I'm not here to ground you!"

Jackson sighed, squared his shoulders, and decided to start over.

"Hello, Simon. It's good to see you. What can I do for you?" said Jackson as calmly as he could manage.

"I've been trying to get Phyllis alone all week. Who are all these people in the house? What's going on? What's today's date?" said Simon, his questions coming rapid-fire.

Jackson invited him to have a seat in the living room and caught him up on what had been going on since Lola's birthday party. Simon didn't look surprised. He took out a folded piece of paper from his pocket. Jackson recognized it as a Traveling letter. Simon held it out for Jackson to read.

"I got this last night," he said as Jackson read through the letter.

"Did you leave the Pocket Watch for them to find?" asked Jackson, looking up from the letter.

"No, I dropped it!" answered Simon.

"So where have you been since you dropped it?" asked Jackson, curious to see if Lola and the others had guessed right.

"I've been doing research in the attic, popping in and out of my room and Phyllis', and spending my nights in the London flat," Simon explained.

Jackson nodded and looked at the letter once more. "How about Devlin? Did you send him a key and the marble?"

Simon rubbed his forehead and asked if Jackson had any alcohol in the house. Jackson's eyebrow shot up. He checked his watch. It was eleven-thirty a.m. "I have beer," he ventured. Simon nodded, and

Jackson got up to get him one. It was a little too early for him. Besides, he still had a full day of work to do.

Simon grabbed the bottle and took a long swig. He sighed and said, "Not yet, I haven't."

At Jackson's confused expression, Simon continued. "I've been jumping forward in time a lot and trying to keep track of what's going on. So far, you've been my best source of information."

Jackson wondered if he should get a beer after all. "What do you mean?"

"Try to remember that, technically, it's 2004 for me. When I travel in time, I don't always do it chronologically. I see now that it would have been simpler to keep track of things that way. But there's been a bit of a learning curve in using the Pocket Watch," Simon said, smiling ruefully to himself as though laughing at a private joke.

"About the Watch," interrupted Jackson. "Why did you tell Lola and Phyllis you didn't know how you had managed to Time Travel? Why didn't you show them the Watch? And why did you say you could only Travel to Lola's sixteenth birthday when that has come and gone?"

"I'll get back to that. So, as I was saying, I've been jumping ahead in time and then backtracking until I found a specific moment. You obviously don't remember the conversations I had with you in the future," explained Simon.

Jackson made a silent 'O' with his mouth and sunk lower into the cushions.

"Before I bring the Key and the Marble to Devlin, I need to know if it turned out okay or if I need to do things differently," he said.

Jackson shrugged and said, "So far, so good, I guess."

Simon nodded grimly. "As of today, yes, things are great. But next week, all hell breaks loose!"

Jackson rose and started pacing. "Do I even want to know?" he asked with a pained expression.

"Someone is after the Pocket Watch and Marble," he said. "To be precise, a group of someones."

"Who?" asked Jackson.

"I need a little more time to investigate. The only thing I'm sure of this time is that you are not involved at all," said Simon.

Jackson checked the time and saw it was almost noon.

"Simon, I have to get back to John and take him to the kitchen for lunch with Sally and Marie. Also, Phyllis wants to meet after lunch to plan out the week. The family is going on a mini-vacation this week. Disney, I think. So it'll be just the staff for a couple of days if that helps. Can we continue this conversation later today?" he asked.

Simon nodded. "That sounds perfect. If everyone is having lunch, no one should be in my room. I'll pop in there and catch up with you later," he said as he summoned his door.

After he was gone, Jackson splashed some cold water over his face and headed down to the garage.

CHAPTER 2

SIMON

SIMON DIDN'T WANT to die. Though he knew eternal life might be a bit of a stretch, he thought he was at least entitled to a few more years. He'd tried chemo and radiation. He'd tried an all-fruit diet.

Every time he jumped ahead in time, he found new protocols to try. So far, the only things that were working and easily accessible in 2004 were massive doses of vitamin C and *methylsulfonylmethane*. But it was slow going, and he needed a miracle.

Now that he'd met his daughter and found out he had a son, he was more determined than ever to find a cure.

Whenever he jumped ahead, he always looked in on Jackson. The boy had a good head on his shoulders, and he wasn't quite as emotional as Phyllis and Lola. However, when he'd gotten no further than the spring of 2021, Jackson was nowhere to be found. Instead, he saw that Phyllis had hired a couple who were living in the caretakers' cottage. His apartment didn't look lived in. Perhaps he was in college.

Back in 2020, a quick search for Phyllis had not produced any results. Perhaps she was Traveling or spending time with Boris. He assumed Lola and Devlin were at The Academy. What was strange was that the Mansion had a distinctly vacant feel to it. Everything was clean and dusted. But there were no cookies in the jar in the kitchen, no snacks in the pool house, and no old newspapers in the recycle bin. The house felt empty.

The caretakers had gone home for the day. Simon felt safe wandering around the house. He went to Lola's room, grabbed her laptop, and headed for the bathroom. This was the only room Jackson had said was safe from the video feeds. If John had taken over for Jackson, Simon would need to be more careful. He made a note to check in with the attorney.

Meanwhile, he went online to search for new cancer treatments. There didn't seem to be anything new. Then, he searched for pages relating to the effects of Time Travel. Besides the usual sci-fi websites, he sometimes found interesting psychology or philosophy doctorate candidates who were studying the ethics and effects of trying to change the outcome of a past event. He'd had many fascinating discussions over the years.

He hadn't shared his discovery of the Pocket Watch, his jumps through time, or his search for a cure with Phyllis. He didn't want to get her hopes up. He also was hoping he could find a cure, go back in time, and nip it in the bud. Now that he knew Elaine, Lola's mother, had died of cancer, he wanted to share the cure with her. But he needed to know more about the implications of such actions. If she didn't die, Lola wouldn't move to Virginia. Perhaps she might have come on her own when she received his letter on her eighteenth birthday. But that event had started a chain of events leading to the Academy and Devlin.

He had considered taking the cure when he found it and going back in time after his death to resume his life incognito, but that seemed overly complicated for his family members. There was also the option of embracing his death, but that went against every fiber in his body. Aside from wanting to spend time with his children, Simon had a thirst for uncovering mysteries.

Finding the Pocket Watch all those years ago in one of the study's hidden compartments had been a stroke of luck. In a moment of anger and despair following yet another round of grueling yet unsuccessful chemotherapy, Simon had struck the wood paneling with his fist while leaning against the bookcase. He'd heard a slight pop and felt the outline of the small drawer protruding.

Momentarily shocked out of his pity party, he'd kneeled to investigate. Sure enough, there was a hidden compartment. Gingerly, he pulled it open to reveal a velour pouch. It was heavy. Pulling apart the drawstrings, he found what looked like an antique gold pocket watch. It was stunning. The carving was intricate and beautiful but also revealed its true ancestry. It was clearly an Evers heirloom. Why was it hidden in the compartment? Was it valuable beyond its worth in gold?

Simon put the Watch back in the pouch and pocketed it. He would examine it later. For now, he was obsessed with looking for other hidden compartments. When Phyllis came in for a nightcap and to read by the fire, he had to halt his explorations. They always enjoyed this time together.

They were both Traveling a lot back then, often missing meals at home. This was their special time. Even when all they did was read in companionable silence. He often wondered if it was odd for two thirty-something people to hang out at home every night with their sibling, enjoying a glass of brandy. It really didn't matter.

It had taken Simon a whole week to search the study. He found two more hidden compartments in the bookcase. He found another under one of the hardwood floor slats under the carpet in front of the fireplace. Yet another when he twisted one of the carved lion heads on the mantle.

When he wasn't in the study, he was in his room studying the Pocket Watch. It became apparent that it was a device used for Time Travel. Though curious by nature, Simon had never been overly studious. However, he was now motivated to find out as much as possible about the timepiece and how to use it. Time Travel would solve so many of his problems!

He Traveled to all the major libraries in the world, then the ones at universities, then bookstores and shops that dealt with Arcane and Magical topics. He eventually struck gold in Bethlehem, Pennsylvania, at a small bookstore called Moravian Bookshop. Not only did the bookstore have a wide selection of relevant books, but Simon's repeated visits had piqued one of the clerks' curiosity. Every time Simon appeared, she had a selection of books set aside to show him. He had told her he was a graduate student working on a thesis on antiques rumored to have magical abilities. Whether she believed him or not, her help had been invaluable.

Once, while he was looking over her latest findings, she approached him and introduced him to Shawna. Shawna was also an undergraduate, and she was studying magical artifacts. Shawna was younger than Simon by a few years. He put her at about twenty-two. They shook hands, and the clerk went back to work.

"So what's your deal?" she asked after Nathalie, the clerk, had gone.

"I beg your pardon, ma'am?" replied Simon with his thickest southern accent.

"Save your southern charm for Nathalie. I ain't biting. There's no such thing as an undergraduate degree in anything magical," she said, hands on her hips.

"So what are you really studying, then?" asked Simon, a look of innocent bewilderment on his face.

"I'm not a student, and I'm willing to bet neither are you," she stated, taking in his expensive clothing. "This here ain't a library, and them books ain't cheap," she said, moving the top book so she could see the title of the book beneath. "Ain't no way a student could afford them."

Simon took a moment to observe his accuser. She was pretty, but she seemed intent on hiding it. Her chestnut hair was straight and hung loosely down her back. She wore no makeup and no jewelry. Her attire was very non-descript: a pair of jeans, leather boots, a belt, and a gray t-shirt. Though she acted nonchalantly, she seemed much too interested in Simon's books. He straightened the pile and picked up the books.

"I really don't see how that's any of your business," he answered, heading towards the registers. "Good day, ma'am."

"It is if you want my help," she said as he passed.

Simon stopped, turned, and smiled. "And why pray tell, would I need your help?" he asked as loftily as he could manage.

She shrugged and looked at her non-existent nails. "Because I know someone who can tell you how to use your Watch," she said, looking up and meeting his eyes.

That got his attention. He debated asking which Watch. She raised an eyebrow as though reading his thoughts. In the end, all he could say was, "Tell me more."

It turned out that the person Shawna was referring to was her girl-friend, Professor Emma Ballantyne. They had to be discreet because theirs was a twice-forbidden relationship. First, because the LGBT movement had a way to go before lesbians could come out in academia. And second, because though there were no laws against consensual workplace relationships at the time, dating one's subordinates was frowned upon.

Once she saw that Simon posed no threat to either her relationship or her university position, Shawna introduced him to Emma.

CHAPTER 3

LIANON

SUMMERSET ISLE WAS STILL one of the most beautiful places Lianon had ever visited. Now that he spent most of his time at the Academy, the Headmaster truly appreciated coming home. He usually made it home for two weeks after the fall semester and for a month after the Summer program. Then typically stayed at the Academy after the winter term to prepare for the summer program and the next fall program. Lady Samsara went home after the winter term, then took another two weeks off after the Summer program. She oversaw whatever came up before the term began, and the Headmaster returned.

The world the Ancients had created for the Academy was purposefully made small, so the students would feel secure and be easily accounted for.

There was never this feeling of spaciousness and purity on Earth, where there were indeed some magical places. Lianon loved humans, but they had a habit of destroying their habitat even when they had the best intentions.

Summerset was a place that humans did not get to visit very often, and if they did, it was never for very long. But those who came were awestruck. Not only because of the lush greenery, the pristine bodies of water, and the unmarred sky. But also for the sheer size of it—a world made for giants.

Adult High Elves grew to seven feet tall. The Ancient Elves often reached nine feet. All of the dwellings and communal spaces had high doorways and ceilings. The trees rose about twelve feet. Wild creatures roamed freely. Though most were friendly, some were so large they could inadvertently crush a human on their way.

He'd only just sat down to play the harp when he was summoned to the High Council. *Now what?*

He rose and cast a mournful look at his instrument and walked over to the Council Edifice. It was a short walk as his dwelling was near the center. When he arrived, he greeted his fellow High Elves and the Ancients who served on the Council.

Saruir, the current Council Leader, beckoned him to sit down and motioned for him to look at the wall. Immediately the stone surface transformed into a screen with a pulsing blue dot. That meant Earth. Saruir waved a hand, and the dot zoomed to Earth, then to North America, then the United States. Lianon's head dropped towards his lap. He had a feeling he knew where this was going. The map kept zooming until it reached the outskirts of Williamsburg, Virginia.

Before Saruir could say anything, Lianon rose and put a hand up. "I shall return presently."

He went towards the same wall, and with a wave of his hand, it transformed into a portal, and he stepped through. He was gone for about twenty minutes. As a security precaution, he headed to his office at the Academy and from there to the Evers Mansion. The children were amazed to see him; that was evident. After proper chastising, Lianon went back to his office, then to the Council to report on his expedition.

"Do you think they will hand over the artifacts?" asked Aeriearie, one of the younger members of the Council.

Lianon shook his head. "I do not think so. Though I've made every effort to gain their trust, the fact is they are still very young and have no one to guide them adequately."

"What about the aunt, Phyllis? Is she not a suitable guardian? Should we appoint another?" asked Saruir.

"I've met with her a handful of times. She's a lovely woman and a suitable guardian in the sense that she loves her niece and nephew and will do everything she can to ensure their well-being and happiness," replied Lianon. "But as she has never attended the Academy and knows nothing of the Travelers' history or heritage, she is in no position to offer magical guidance, as it were. I was hoping to fill that role until they arrived for the fall term."

"Perhaps it should have been mandatory for her to attend the Summer program as well," ventured Rumena. This got a few chuckles from the assembly.

"I've given her a copy of the Traveler's Handbook, and I presume the children will update her on the most important aspects of magic. What worries me is the fact that none of them seem to know who to trust. Phyllis was kidnapped a few months ago, and only last week, Devlin's townhouse was ransacked. They are understandably wary of anyone who takes an interest in their artifacts, including me."

"Have they no other guidance?" asked Saruir.

"They have attorneys. I've spoken to both Radcliffs. At first, they were not very forthcoming. We had concluded ample research and were able to trace their involvement with the very first Evers in Williamsburg: Lord John Evers. Phyllis provided us with a copy of their family tree. What was odd is that Lord Evers had a single child, a female named Emmeline Evers. Per human customs of the time, she should have taken her husband's name. But on the family tree, her husband is recorded as Archibald Evers. As it was also commonplace for cousins to marry in those days, we assumed that was the case but could find no record of an Archibald Evers. More efforts were deployed, and we found their marriage certificate. Emmeline Rose Evers wed Archibald Phineous Langly on April 21, 1698."

Lianon stopped talking as he heard the collective gasps around the room.

"Langly! Isn't he the one who disappeared from the Council of Elders and was never found?" asked Rumena.

"Did he not die of the plague with his wife and child?" asked Aeriearie.

"It would appear not. And I would venture a guess that he had the Archivum copied or translated into English at some point because the Evers have their very own copy. I requested an appointment with the Evers' attorney. Once I shared our findings with them, they became cooperative. It seems they have a magic vault in their offices. It's where the Evers' Repository, Archives, Time Watch, and Sphere reside when not in use by the Custodian. It's really very well made. I was unable to breach it."

Saruir was stroking his silver-white beard. "This leads to many more questions," he said. "Were the attorneys able to shed any light on the provenance of their magical safe?"

"It seems the first Mr. Radcliff, George, was quite taken with Lady Emmeline, but she had refused his interest. Because of attorney-client confidentiality, Lady Emmeline chose him as a confidant. George Radcliff kept detailed notes of each of his meetings with all of his clients. All his meetings with Lord Evers were about the Estate. However, his meetings with Lady Emmeline revealed a fantastical tale.

"Her mother, Rose Analise Evers, née Harding, was a witch. She died in childbirth in 1683. The child, a son, did not survive. Miss Rosetta Foley, Emmeline's nurse, was also a witch and was later replaced by a governess named Sara Sharp, also a witch. From Mr. Radcliff's notes, it appears Lord Evers remained unaware that both his wife and daughter, as well as their entourage of servants, were witches. When Lady Emmeline married Archibald Langly, she was only sixteen years old but already proved to be a masterful witch. Perhaps that is why she was able to keep her father and most people in the dark. She did, however, reveal herself to her husband after he had changed his name and impregnated her. He took it well. It seems he then revealed himself as a Traveler and confessed the events that had led him to the Colonies. Upon hearing her husband's tale, Lady Emmeline commissioned an iron vault, which she later enchanted.

"The vault, installed in the Radcliff's offices to ensure the contents were away from the Evers Mansion should it ever be seized or searched, held the Evers artifacts and other small items of value. The enchantment made it so that any authorized Radcliff attorney could access the contents on behalf of their Evers clients."

"How would they know if a Radcliff attorney was authorized?" asked Rumena.

"It's actually a rather simple spell," replied Lianon, clearly impressed. "The enchantment covered both the turnover of new Radcliff attorneys and new Evers Custodians. Whenever it was time for either of the roles to be handed down to the next in line, a short ceremony would occur. I do not have the details, as it is a secret ceremony, but it involves placing a hand on the Archivum and reciting an Incantation."

"Fascinating," said Saruir, and the others nodded in agreement.

"She also enchanted the artifacts so they could be teleported to and from the safe by the Custodian," added Lianon.

"A clever addition, not unlike how the keys are returned to the Repository when lost or revoked," interjected Aeriearie in amusement. "It seems Archibald aligned himself with a good witch. Were the artifacts misused by the pair?"

"He never used the Sphere, and there is no way to know if he used the Time Watch for good or ill. Also, they had very little time together, as Lady Emmeline died in childbirth," replied Lianon.

Rumena perused the Ancestry and asked, "What became of the twins, Oleander and Anemone? Did they have their mother's magical abilities?"

"The journals made no mention of their magical abilities. I believe a fellow witch may have bound their powers shortly after their birth. Or perhaps the Radcliffs chose not to divulge this information. Oleander became the next Custodian, and the journals chronicle his dealings with George, then his son George Junior."

The Council discussed the Evers at length, and many suggestions were made, though no decisions were made. In the end, they agreed. It was time to extend an invitation to the Evers family.

CHAPTER 4

EDWARD

EDWARD DIDN'T KNOW what to make of the Headmaster. The man kept sending letters of inquiry and requesting meetings. At first, the attorney had answered general questions at the behest of his client, Ms. Phyllis Evers. But now, the Headmaster was digging into the Radcliff ancestry, insinuating things were not above board.

When Edward went into practice with his father, he was told nothing about the magical nature of the Evers' affairs. He was instructed to accept the unexplained as fact and that further information would be provided if and when it became necessary to do so. He understood that some clients choose to keep their business close to the chest and attorneys need to live with mysteries. After all, it is not an attorney's place to understand or pass judgment on their client's dealings. It was, however, an attorney's responsibility to protect their clients, safeguard their secrets, and ensure they complied with the letter of the law.

With time, the senior Radcliff provided more and more context until, ten years before his retirement, he gave Edward the journals belonging to George Radcliff. They were ancient, handwritten, and a chore to decipher. But reading all twenty-five of them was the condition for taking over his father's firm. And so Edward read, looking up ancient terms and making notes to ask his father about. Since he was also busy building the business, acquiring new clients, and establishing a family, the task took him nearly five years.

When he was done, his father opened their family safe and produced journals for every single Radcliff lawyer who came after George, including his own. Edward's stomach dropped. There had to be at least fifty journals in there! He hoped his father was not about to impose yet another condition before handing over the firm to him.

"You will need to document your dealings relating to the Evers family," said Edward Sr.

Edward Jr. looked warily at the journals stacked in the safe, then back at his father.

"And read all your predecessors' journals, including mine, of course," added his father, patting the leather-bound notebooks fondly.

"Of course," replied Edward stiffly.

Now he understood why his father had disclosed this information ten years before his retirement. It seems the Evers paid the bulk of their retainer. In fact, theirs was a perpetual retainer. Provisions had been made to retain their firm forever.

"Evers *are* Forever," mused Edward, as he took in the complicated investments whose dividends poured directly into the Radcliff's business account at Burke & Herbert Bank & Trust Co.—the oldest bank in Virginia.

Clearly, the Evers were their most important client. Edward made time every day to read through the journals. He was forty years old by the time he had read all the way through his father's journals. Most had proved uneventful and rather boring compared to those of George Radcliff. It was partly due to the nature of George's interaction with Lady Emmeline. The others had few magical anecdotes, if any, to impart. He was determined to make his own journals as interesting as possible while being clear and succinct. Surely his own son, or daughter, would appreciate his efforts. But what if neither of them wanted to follow in his footsteps? Times had changed. No matter, he would write diligently and hope his successor, whoever it may be, would continue the tradition.

Here he was, twenty years later. Things were getting interesting again, but he had no one except his near-senile father to share them with. Surely he couldn't be the last Radcliff? Neither of his children had gone into law. Elsbeth was now a biochemist. Though he wasn't entirely sure how she spent her days, he was quite proud of her. Finnigan was a Philosophy professor at Raleigh. He was a fine young man. None of the firm's associates seemed likely candidates to take up such a longstanding and discreet tradition.

When Headmaster Lianon started pestering him, Edward began thinking this might be the opportunity to pass on the baton, so to speak. The High Elves lived very long lives, and the Headmaster clearly knew all about Travelers, Keys, antique Pocket Watches, and whatever that odd-looking Marble did. Edward was tired. He wanted to retire, like his father before him. At sixty years old, he felt he was entitled to his hard-earned rest.

Edward picked up the phone and dialed the number on Headmaster Lianon's card. The 800-number was dispatched to an automated voice messaging service.

"Headmaster Lianon, this is Edward Radcliff Jr. If you are available, I would be happy to meet with you at our offices in Williamsburgh on August 17 at ten a.m.," he said and hung up.

Edward made an entry in his journal and rose to place the journal back in the vault. Upon his return, he saw a familiar envelope resting on his desk. Sliding the letter opener through the top, he found the Headmaster's short handwritten acceptance of the proposed meeting time.

CHAPTER 5

TOM

WHAT AN UNGODLY HOUR, thought Tom, quickly silencing his watch so he wouldn't wake the others. *The things you do for love!*

A smile crept across his face but disappeared quickly. His head ached. He and the guys had crawled into the bunks at around three a.m. and swiftly passed out. Which was good, because he probably couldn't have fallen asleep with all that snoring.

Gingerly, he climbed down the ladder as quietly as he could. But as he got to the floor, he realized Devlin wasn't in his bed. Getting up early had to be a family thing, he mused. He hoped Devlin and Lola weren't meditating together. That was the whole point of the escapade, to spend time alone with Lola. To surprise her with a cup of coffee and a view of the Channel.

He grabbed his t-shirt, jeans, and shoes from the pile on the floor and crept out of the room. Heading to the kitchen, he tried to think if he had ever gotten up this early before. It certainly was quiet, even with so many guests in the house. He made a pot of coffee, and reluctantly prepared three travel cups, in case he had to offer one to Devlin.

Placing the cups on a small tray, he went out through the patio doors and onto the deck. They weren't by the pool, or on the lawn beyond it. He headed down the path to the Channel. It was a beautiful morning; the sun rising out of the water to greet him. But other than a lone fisherman, there was no one else to greet him.

Frowning, he stalked back towards the house. He abandoned his tray on a table in the foyer and tiptoed to the girls' bunkroom. Easing the door open, he popped his head into the room. Only three beds were occupied; no Lola. He closed the door gently and headed back to the boys' room. Devlin wasn't back.

Where are they? They must have gone exploring. It was much too early to worry his mother and uncle, and he was tired. He stripped down to his underwear, made his way to the top bunk, and promptly fell back asleep.

CHAPTER 6

JACKSON

JACKSON WAS PACING. He'd arrived in the Evers' London flat yesterday as planned. It was an awesome location, less than five minutes from the tube. After a quick nap and a shower, he set off for the pub to meet with his friends. They'd had a great time talking about their high school days and catching up on what they'd been doing since. He was happy to see that life wasn't all girls and parties for these guys. The cognitive science program they were enrolled in was brutal and, though they were having the time of their lives, the guys said it took up most of their time.

They had parted company around midnight. Jackson explained he was catching an early train the next day, and the guys had to go into the lab, anyway. He promised to drop by their lab for a visit before he went back home to America.

It was now five a.m. on Sunday and he was waiting for news from Simon. It was going down; whatever 'it' was. Lola and Devlin were attending a party in Ireland. According to Simon, things went south sometime between nine and eleven p.m., Virginia time. They had discussed it at length while Phyllis and the kids were at Disney. The only way of preventing the events that followed, of which Simon had provided numerous details, was to intervene as they happened in the Evers Mansion.

They had not informed Phyllis of their plan. It was easier for her to go to Boris', as planned, after dropping the kids off at the party. The house would be empty and the culprit or culprits would be free to roam, seemingly undetected and unobserved. To be on the safe side, Jackson had gifted John and Sally a pair of tickets to a play in town, saying he had forgotten he'd purchased them and didn't want them to go to waste. There was no one on the Evers Estate.

CHAPTER 7
SIMON

SIMON STARED at the video feeds on Jackson's computers. At nine p.m., three men appeared outside the mudroom door. He recognized one of them: it was Donatelli.

"Bastard," said Simon to the screen.

One of the men hung back and seemed to be keeping watch. The other man waved something in front of the keypad and somehow managed to get the door opened. They both waited before crossing the threshold. The other man then waved at the security console and the alarm was disabled. Simon held his breath; would the man also disable the cameras? But he only gave a nod and gestured for Donatelli to enter. He looked at his watch and said something before turning to the third man and nodding to him. The third man produced a door, and they left.

Donatelli did a quick tour of the main floor and began his search in the Study. He was methodical and precise, leaving things as they were. After about thirty minutes, he seemed to sigh in exasperation and left the room. He quickly went from room to room but did not give the main floor rooms more than a cursory search.

He moved to the second floor and started with a guest room, then Devlin's, then Lola's. Then a quick search in the gym and nursery before heading to Simon's room. He stayed quite a while in Simon's room. There, he found Simon's signet ring and began writing a letter at his desk. He folded it and sent it off.

Next, he went to Phyllis' room. He gave it a thorough search but still did not seem to find what he was looking for. At one point he stopped abruptly and reached into his pocket. He took out a cell phone. As Simon peered closer, he recognized Phyllis' flowery case.

"What the devil are you doing with Phyllis' phone?" exclaimed Simon, rising now, but keeping his eyes glued on the screen. The man smiled at what he saw and quickly sent back a reply.

He seemed very pleased with himself and went to sit at Phyllis' vanity table. Reaching into his jacket, he produced a gun, which he set on his lap and waited.

This is it. Simon pulled out his Key and the door appeared. He checked the time on the screen; it was ten p.m. He took out the cell phone Jackson had given him and sent him a quick text to let him know it was about to go down.

CHAPTER 8
DEVLIN

"I THINK you know what I want. The Watch and the Marble, if you please," said the man, casually waving the gun at them.

Lola reached for him with her mind. *What do we do?* she asked.

We need to stall or distract him. I'm sure we'll think of something, was Devlin's reply.

"We do not have them," said Devlin to the man. "They are in a safe at our attorney's office."

The man smiled and nodded, getting up while still pointing the gun at them.

"And it's Saturday, so the offices are closed," added Lola.

"Do you take me for a fool?" asked the man, his accent getting thicker as he took a step closer. "I'm told that you can call them to you. Are you not the Custodian?"

Devlin's face fell. "Yes, I am the Custodian."

"Wait," interjected Lola. "You sound Italian, are you Donatelli?" she asked the man.

"That is of no concern of yours," he replied as he moved the barrel of the gun in her direction and cocked the pistol. "Devlin, unless you want me to shoot your sister, call the artifacts forth immediately."

Devlin raised both hands, palm upwards, and closed his eyes as though in silent meditation. In truth, he was playing for time. He wondered if perhaps he could call the repository instead. The box wouldn't open for the man and he could claim it was a mistake and try again, calling the book next, as it would not open for anyone but him and would be useless to the man. He was thinking out loud in his mind, keeping Lola apprised of his ideas and waiting for her to come up with her own.

In the end, he did none of those things. Because a door appeared between the man and them. A man walked out, grabbed their hands, and pulled them through the opening. It was over in seconds. Devlin didn't recognize the room they were in. He turned to see that Lola was embracing the man. This was his father.

CHAPTER 9
LOLA

"DAD!" she exclaimed and jumped into his arms. "I thought I'd never see you again."

Simon wrapped his arms around her and held her tight. She burrowed her face into his shirt and inhaled the scent of him, holding him tighter like he might disappear if she didn't tether him to her.

After a moment, he released her and faced Devlin. Lola looked at her father, then at Devlin. Neither spoke, but both held matching thunderstruck expressions.

Lola cleared her throat and said, "Allow me to do the introductions. Dad, this is Devlin, your son. Devlin, this is our dad."

Simon took a step towards his son and waited. Devlin took a step and held out his hand.

"It is an honor to finally meet you," said Devlin, a bit stiffly, his voice hoarse.

Simon smiled and clasped his hand. "Indeed, it's an honor for me as well, Devlin."

They stood for a moment, joined by a handshake until Simon pulled him in and gave him a hug. The men were the same height and stature, though Simon was thinner.

Lola could see tears running down both their faces. As endearing as it was, it was also a bit creepy. It had never occurred to her that her father didn't look old enough to have teenage children. Though he would have been in his late forties had he been alive, the man who stood before her was in his thirties.

They finally broke apart, both of them trying to regain their composure.

"I don't mean to break up this lovely family reunion, but I think we should discuss what just happened," said Lola.

"Quite right, darling," said Simon, stroking Lola's hair as he looked at her.

He took out his Key, opened the door, and beckoned for them to follow.

CHAPTER 10
JACKSON

JACKSON HEARD the beep and knew the text was from Simon. *It's happening*, was all it said. They had agreed to meet here, whether or not Simon was successful. All Jackson could do was wait. He made a fresh pot of coffee and set out some snacks. Phyllis would want him to be a good host, regardless of the circumstances. He shook his head and rolled his shoulders, willing himself to relax.

In the blink of an eye, a door appeared, and out came Simon, then Lola and Devlin. *I need to get used to this*, he thought. Before he knew what he was doing, he strode to Lola and wrapped her in a tight hug.

"Thank god you're okay," he breathed into her hair.

Lola hugged him back lightly.

"Sorry," he said quietly as he pulled back. They'd never dated but he was the one that had broken off their unofficial relationship; Lola might not appreciate his feelings right now. Facing Devlin and Simon, he said, "Are you alright?"

"Yes, we are all fine. Thank you for asking," replied Devlin, taking in his surroundings.

Seeing Devlin's confusion, Simon spoke up. "We're at the London flat, we're safe here."

They all grabbed cups of coffee and sat down in the living room.

Simon updated them on what he'd seen on the video feeds, then explained to Lola and Devlin what he and Jackson had been up to during the last week. Lola and Devlin shared what had happened with the Sphere and the Headmaster.

"Devlin, could you call the book and the artifacts, please," asked Simon.

Devlin asked for the Archives, the Pocket Watch, the Sphere, and the Repository. In quick succession, the items landed on the coffee table. Though Lola and Devlin had seen this happen before, they both smiled at Jackson's audible gasp. They all stared at the artifacts and waited for Simon to provide further instructions.

"Good, everything is as it should be. Since I'm no longer the Custodian, Devlin will need to proceed from here," said Simon, smiling at Devlin.

"What should I do?" asked Devlin, perplexed.

"Nothing, just yet. We need to figure out what's going on," replied Simon.

"From what you've said, it appears that Donatelli is working with two accomplices," ventured Jackson. "One of them was there simply to give them a ride, so to speak. Donatelli's Key has likely been revoked by his Custodian because he kidnapped Phyllis. The third man must be a wizard, or whatever, and probably the man your Headmaster was referring to. Though they don't seem to have Traveled without a Key. Unless he was using tiny tech you couldn't see on the screen, he was using magic to disable the security system."

"Right, but how did they get Phyllis' phone?" asked Lola. "She wouldn't leave for a weekend at Boris' without it, especially if Devlin and I were at a house party in Ireland. She would be too worried that something might happen, and we'd need to get in touch with her."

"Perhaps they stole it from her while she was at Boris'?" suggested Devlin.

"Or perhaps Boris is part of the band of accomplices," said Jackson.

They all fell silent as they pondered this fact. Simon nodded his head, his expression grim.

"The thought did occur to me, as well. But she and Boris had a longstanding relationship before this all happened. It's no big surprise that after we found out he was also a Traveler, their relationship would bloom into something more serious. And he was a great help in recovering her during the kidnapping. I really don't think Boris is a bad guy," concluded Simon.

"Then perhaps we should contact him to make sure Phyllis is alright," suggested Devlin.

"Yes, but in a way that won't alarm Phyllis or make Boris suspicious if he is involved," countered Jackson, still not convinced about Boris' innocence.

"I could call him and ask to speak to Phyllis. Saying I tried her cell and she didn't pick up," ventured Lola. "He won't ask why, but if he does, I'll say I'm not feeling well and was thinking of going home early or something."

"Yes, good idea, Lola," was Simon's response.

Lola took out her phone and dialed Boris' number, but paused before tapping the handset icon. "It's really early, and on a Sunday," she said.

"If you were sick and calling your parent, this would not be an issue," said Devlin.

"Yes, you're right," she replied and made the call. Putting the phone to her ear, she waited for Boris to pick up. He answered on the second ring, sounding very much awake.

"Um, Boris, it's Lola. I'm sorry to bother you so early, but can I speak to my aunt? She isn't picking up her cell phone..." said Lola in what she hoped sounded like the voice of an unsure teenager.

"Lola, is everything alright?" he asked immediately, with obvious concern.

"Yes, well, no. I'd really like to talk to Phyllis," she insisted.

"Yes, of course. I'll go wake her up. Give me a moment," he replied.

"Thank you, Boris," said Lola.

Lola put her hand over the phone and whispered, "He's going to wake her up."

They waited.

Devlin got up to grab some food from the counter and a glass of water. He told the others his head was killing him and went to the bathroom to see if he could find pain medication. He'd had too much to drink and not enough sleep. He found some in the vanity and popped a couple of pills before heading back to the living room.

When he got back, Lola was still waiting for Phyllis to come on the line. Then her face lit up as she exclaimed "Phyllis!" After which she bit her lip and said, "No, I'm fine. Devlin's fine too, though to be honest I think he had a bit too much to drink and we were thinking of heading home early instead of staying through the brunch. Is that okay?"

They waited as Lola listened to her aunt's response. "Um, sure, hold on," she said, holding the phone out to Devlin and mouthing 'sorry' to him as he took it.

"Hello, Phyllis... Yes, I am fine... I know. I am sorry. I have learned my lesson... No, Lola went to bed early, at eleven... I think I went to bed at three in the morning... Yes, I have taken a large glass of water and a pain reliever... Of course. All is well with you and Boris?"

From his pained expression and his side of the conversation, it was clear Phyllis was giving Devlin the 'I'm so disappointed in you' speech, which was so much worse than being yelled at. Jackson knew that all too well.

Devlin concluded the call by saying he'd see her for Sunday dinner and that he and Lola would stay home and take it easy for the rest of the day.

"I do not like lying to her," he said, handing the phone back to Lola.

"I'm sorry I made you the scapegoat," blurted Lola.

"That is fine. I am the older brother, and I am over eighteen. I should know better," he said.

Simon nodded appreciatively and clasped a hand on Devlin's shoulder. "Good man. What did Phyllis say when you asked if everything was alright? We got the gist of the rest of your conversation," he added wryly.

"She said she and Boris had gone to the theater last night and had planned to stay in this morning. She'll be home around four p.m. to start dinner. I don't think she is aware that anything is amiss," answered Devlin.

"And, she told me she thought she'd forgotten her phone at home, and was sorry she'd missed my call," added Lola.

They took a moment to process this information.

"For now, I'm satisfied that Boris is not involved, and that Phyllis is safe where she is," said Simon. Everyone nodded in agreement.

"We know Donatelli is working with at least two other people. They seem to be the likely suspects. How do we feel about the Headmaster and The Academy?" asked Lola.

"I don't know about you, but I'm inclined to trust a High Elf who's been around for a lot longer than we have," said Simon.

"Yes, I agree. If it appeared they were trying to take the artifacts from us, it might have been because they do not trust us with them. Which, of course, is completely understandable because of our ancestor Archibald," replied Devlin.

Jackson frowned. "Can someone fill me in here? Who is Archibald?"

Lola and Devlin gave him a summary of what they had found out from the Archives. Simon told them about his visits to Archibald in the past, and the bits and pieces he had gleaned from studying the book. He was clearly surprised to learn that you could ask the book questions instead of searching for it. He agreed that would provide much faster answers.

"Can you show me?" asked Jackson tentatively.

Devlin looked at Lola and Simon for confirmation. "He's come this far," said Lola, shrugging.

"I trust Jackson completely, and so does Phyllis," said Simon.

Devlin faced the book. "What shall I ask?"

"Perhaps ask if it knows the location of the High Elves' world since that is where they are tracking the Marbles from," suggested Simon.

Devlin thought a moment and asked, "How do I get to Summerset Isle?"

The book seemed to vibrate a bit and then the cover flew open and the pages started flipping very quickly before settling on a blank page. They all moved closer and saw text appear on it.

Jackson had been taking this whole Traveling business in stride, but a magical book that wrote out answers to questions was another thing entirely. He moved even closer and started to read over Devlin's shoulder.

Summerset Isle is the homeland of the Ancient and High Elves. Located on planet Nirn, specifically on the Tamriel continent. Within Nirn, it can be reached by water. Elves usually use portals to transport them to and from their homeland. Travelers require the use of a Sphere. Getting to Summerset is simply a matter of intending it as you place the Sphere in the door socket.

"That sounds simple enough," shot Jackson with a wink.

"Father, where did you go when you used the Sphere?" asked Devlin.

"How do you know I used the Sphere?" asked Simon, surprised.

"The book told us. It said the only two Evers who had used it were Devlin and Simon," replied Lola.

"Where did you go?" asked Jackson, eyes huge, facing Devlin.

"I didn't go anywhere. We were flipping through worlds when Headmaster Lianon intercepted us and explained why that was a bad idea," said Devlin with a chuckle.

Lola gave a shudder and explained how they might have let monsters into their world had he not arrived when he did.

"Wouldn't the Elves have some sort of protection to keep unwanted people out of their world?" asked Jackson.

"Good point," said Simon. "But since they automatically know when a Sphere is being used, I'm assuming they would be warned when it is being used by a human to enter their world."

"I mean, we have to try, right? They are the closest thing we have to calling the police," said Lola.

"What about the Council of Elders?" asked Jackson.

"Because of Donatelli's involvement, I feel like the Council may have been breached. Or, at the very least, may not be all that sympathetic to our cause, considering we are the descendants of a thief..." said Simon.

"I agree," said Devlin. "The Elves have no stake in this beyond ensuring the artifacts are being used correctly. By going directly to them, are we not showing our willingness to comply?"

"Yes, you're right. And now the big question," said Lola, looking at each of them in turn.

"Who's going to Summerset Isle?" asked Jackson.

CHAPTER II

TOM

EVERYONE WAS ASSEMBLED under the canopy, filling plates, drinking mimosas, and discussing the previous night's festivities. Clearly, it had been a hit and Tom was sure people would be talking about his party for years to come. He should have been elated; his social reputation was golden.

Lola and Devlin's absence had definitely dampened his euphoria. In fact, he was quite worried. He'd awoken with the others and stumbled outside for coffee and to greet his guests. There had been no time to let his mother and uncle know about his early morning venture. Hoping beyond all hope that Lola and Devlin would already be outside. But they weren't. They were nowhere to be found. And now it seemed his mother and uncle had noticed and were heading his way.

"A word, Tom?" said his uncle, grabbing a firm hold of his arm as he dragged him away from his friends towards the house.

"Where are Lola and Devlin?" asked his mother.

"I don't know," he replied honestly.

"What do you mean you don't know?" replied his uncle, shaking his arm before letting it go.

"I woke early this morning so I could be alone with Lola. She's up with the sun and likes to meditate," he explained. "But I couldn't find her anywhere, nor could I find Devlin."

"Why did you not come and see us immediately?" asked his mother. "What if they're hurt or ill?"

"It was five a.m. and I was tired. I figured they'd gone for a walk and would turn up at brunch like everyone else," he said defensively.

"Call Lola on her mobile. Ask if she's alright," ordered Aidan.

"I was about to do that anyhow. Why is this such a big deal?" asked Tom. "What's so important about Lola and Devlin; are they some kind of royalty?"

Aidan and his mother looked at one another but did not respond. When his uncle had suggested he get close to Lola at school, he'd thought the request was odd, but as Lola was gorgeous and adorable, it was an easy enough task. He'd figured his uncle wanted him to make friends with Lola because she was an heiress. His mother was always telling him he needed to choose a wealthy bride to ensure the family's continued prosperity. He'd stopped objecting to this outdated notion when his father died, and his mother would start to cry when he told her he would marry for love.

He had fallen in love with Lola, but as they were only sixteen, surely it was too early to be talking about uniting their families with the bonds of marriage?

"What's this really about?" he asked them.

"Lola and Devlin's parents are dead, we need to look out for them," replied his mother.

"They have an aunt, Phyllis. You've met her," replied Tom.

He wasn't buying the concerned act his mother was putting on. First, his mother could barely remember Lola's name after he had introduced her at the picnic. Second, Arabella was a snob; she would never encourage Tom to pursue an American, no matter how rich she was. There was something else going on.

"I won't call her until one of you tells me the truth," said Tom, his voice rising and catching the attention of his guests.

His mother shushed him and led him further away. "Tell him, Aidan. He has the right to know," she said in hushed tones.

"Very well," replied Aidan. "But now is not the time for a lengthy explanation. Your guests are waiting."

"Fine, I'll call her to see if she's okay," he said.

Tom took out his phone and dialed Lola's number. She picked up on the third ring.

"Lola, it's Tom. Where are you? Are you alright?"

CHAPTER 12

DEVLIN

"I THINK WE SHOULD ALL GO," said Simon. "I wouldn't feel safe leaving anyone behind. If the door keeps some of us from crossing, then we'll reassess."

They turned expectant eyes towards Devlin. He reached for the carved wooden box and opened it. He eyed the Sphere warily. He'd never felt so nervous in his life. He wondered if they could remain trapped in another World. Or to mistakenly arrive at another destination. That is why he had not objected when Simon suggested they all go together. As cowardly as it was, he did not want to be alone on this journey.

Taking a deep breath, he grabbed the Sphere and stood. He sent the remaining artifacts back to the vault. Should they be successful in their world jump, he didn't know how long they'd be gone.

Looking around him for a little more room, he walked towards the kitchen a few paces before stopping. He turned to look at Simon. His father nodded encouragingly.

Devlin closed his fist around the Sphere and reached for his key. Eyes shut, he thought of Summerset Isle and of Headmaster Lianon. His door appeared with a socket. He placed the Sphere in the socket, waited for it to glow, and then pocketed it as the book had instructed. Before turning the handle, he turned to beckon the others, but they were already right behind him. They each placed a hand on his shoulders or back.

He turned the handle and opened the door. The light on the other side was so bright they all shaded their eyes as they crossed the threshold. This had to be the right place. It looked like paradise. A wild, untamed paradise. It reminded him of the jungle in the movie *Avatar*. Everything was huge. The trees must have been over fifty feet tall, and the bushes as high as the trees back home.

The others were as amazed as he was. Lola ran her fingers over the leaf of one of the flowers. It was the size of a cat. Simon had moved away from them, seemingly looking for something. Perhaps a path out of the jungle.

"What did you intend, or visualize, when summoning the door, Devlin?" asked Simon.

"Summerset Isle and Headmaster Lianon. I figured it would take us to either of them should the Headmaster not be here at present," answered Devlin, hoping he had got it right.

They had lost sight of Jackson and soon heard him bellow, "This way!"

Everyone turned in the direction of his voice but could not see him. There was a rustling as he popped his head out of the bush. "I've found a path or a road of some sort," he said.

They followed him through the thick brush to a wide dirt path. One way led back into the brush. The other led towards what looked like a city. It was breathtaking. In the valley, there was a lake and behind it, they could see houses etched into the hill. Atop the hill was a castle, gleaming in the sunlight.

As though silently agreeing this was their destination, they started walking on the path towards it. The air was pure and crisp, the temperature similar to Stockholm in the Spring, thought Devlin.

They walked the path for about thirty minutes before arriving at the lake. The air was warmer here, and they could smell the lush vegetation that grew around it. It smelled like rain. They stopped near the lake to take in its beauty, but their peaceful contemplation was broken by the sound of what could only be horses approaching.

Turning towards the sound, they saw a carriage pulled by two snow-white horse-like beasts. They stood at least ten feet high. Their hoofs were wooly, like those of shetland ponies, and their manes looked like spun gold. They had no bridles; Devlin could not see any ropes or other tethers between the beasts and the carriage.

The carriage door opened and out came Headmaster Lianon.

"Headmaster!" exclaimed Lola. "Are we happy to see you!"

Lianon approached them, turning first to Simon. Extending his hand, he said, "You must be Simon Evers."

Simon shook his hand. "Guilty as charged," he said, trying to lighten the mood. The Headmaster smiled and nodded to Lola and Devlin. Turning his gaze towards Jackson, he frowned.

"This is Jackson," said Lola. "A good friend of the family." She looped her arm through his as though to say where she went, he went.

"A pleasure to meet you, young man," said Lianon, extending his hand.

"Yes, sir," replied Jackson, awkwardly.

"Come along," said the High Elf, gesturing to the carriage. "We've been expecting you."

CHAPTER 13

SIMON

THE CARRIAGE RIDE WAS BRIEF. They followed the Headmaster into a large, white, domed Pavilion. Once inside, they walked down a large white corridor that led to an outdoor atrium. People, well actually, Elves, were seated on stone benches chatting in pairs or small groups. Conversation halted when their group arrived. Curious glances were sent their way, and Simon assumed the whispers and shocked expressions were due to the fact that they were not used to seeing humans in their midst.

They crossed the atrium and entered through a large frameless glass door that slid open as they approached, then closed when the last of them had passed. Simon could see no hardware or mechanism. It had to be magic.

They walked to the end of an identical corridor and stopped in front of a wall. The Elf raised a hand, and an opening appeared in the wall. They followed him through to a large meeting room where a number of Elves were assembled.

"Members of the Council, may I present Simon, Devlin, and Lola Evers, as well as their good family friend Jackson," said Lianon as solemnly as he could.

The man—*no, Elf,* Simon silently corrected himself—at the head of the table turned towards them and rose.

"Welcome to Summerset Isle. I am Saruir, Leader of the Council of Elves."

Devlin bent at the waist in a bow. Lola curtsied. Simon and Jackson quickly bowed as well. The other Elves at the table rose and took a step back from the table, which immediately lengthened and two extra chairs appeared on either side of the table.

Saruir motioned to the table behind him. "Please, join us."

Lola and Devlin followed the Headmaster to one side of the table. Simon led Jackson to the opposite side and sat opposite his children when the Elves sat down.

Introductions were made, but Simon couldn't remember the names of all the Council members. He did notice that some of the Elves appeared much older than the others and that their attire was different. *These must be the Ancient Elves,* he thought. What he wouldn't give to stay here with them and learn about their history and their customs.

"That can be arranged," said Rumena, seated next to him.

"I beg your pardon?" asked Simon.

"I apologize, was that meant to be a private thought?" she asked, amused.

"Oh, I, ah..." floundered Simon.

She placed a hand on his and winked. "We can discuss it later," she said cheekily.

The Leader, Saruir, told the visitors they had been discussing them and had concluded an invitation should be sent. But here they were—prematurely! He asked them to explain what had prompted their visit.

Simon gave them a summary of what had happened. Lola and Devlin added to the story, and Jackson remained a mute observer. The Headmaster gave them a rundown of his own investigation. Some of the Council members asked questions. Once all the facts were on the table, Saruir took over.

"I'm glad we finally have a full picture. You may rest assured that we will take it from here. We believe the two accomplices you mentioned are Aidan Callahan and Ivan Lazarus."

Both Lola and Devlin gasped.

"Aidan is Tom's uncle and Ivan is his illusionist friend!" exclaimed Lola.

"And how do you come to know these people?" asked Saruir.

"They organized Tom's birthday party. The one we attended last night!" exclaimed Devlin.

"And who is Tom?" asked Aeriearie in confusion.

"Tom Callahan is a student at the Academy," replied Lianon.

"Ivan Lazarus is more than an illusionist," said Saruir. "He's a low-level wizard who's caught the attention of the Council. We've received multiple complaints that he's been misusing his magical abilities on Earth. Since aligning himself with Aidan Callahan, he's had access to a number of high-profile humans. The pair have started a sort of cult, leading their followers to believe they can Travel instantly to anywhere in the world. They initially recruited Travelers to act as 'paid chauffeurs,' but when the Travelers' Keys were revoked for misuse, they had to find another way of keeping their wealthy clients satisfied. We don't know how they did it, but they started creating portals."

"How is that possible? I thought only Elves could open portals. Are they using a Sphere?" asked Simon.

"That is what we aim to find out," replied Saruir. "In the interim, we would like to extend our hospitality to you and your family, including Ms. Phyllis Evers. We have only scratched at the surface of your family's history and abilities. Going forward, I believe you and Ms. Evers may require guidance. As for Lola and Devlin, they will receive adequate training at The Academy regarding the use of the Traveling artifacts. However, it would not be the best place to nurture any other magical abilities that may arise in time. Would you consider staying a fortnight with us?"

Simon looked at Lola and Devlin; they both shrugged.

"I believe we should discuss it as a family. Also, we'll need to deliver young Jackson here back to London so he may resume his activities," said Simon, placing a hand on Jackson's shoulder.

Saruir nodded in understanding. "Of course. Send us a Traveling Letter on the morrow with your answer."

When he rose, the other Council members followed suit. Saruir nodded to Lianon, who gestured for the group to follow him. They made their way to the stone wall at the back of the room, expecting to see an opening form as it had upon entering the room.

The Headmaster waved at the wall, and a huge circular portal appeared. "Where are you going?" he asked Simon. Simon gave him the address of the London flat and they saw the living room through the waterfall shimmer of the portal. "Safe Travels," he said and nodded for them to proceed through the portal. When the last of their group had crossed, the portal disappeared.

CHAPTER 14

LOLA

IT WAS eleven-thirty when they got back to the London flat. They nibbled at the snacks that Jackson had laid out in the morning and warmed up the coffee.

"I guess we'll need to discuss this with Phyllis at dinner tonight," said Lola with a yawn.

"Yes, and there is not much we can do right this minute. Surely the intruders have left by now. Perhaps we could go home and get some rest. It has been a long night," replied Devlin.

"Indeed," agreed Simon. "Let me pop back to make sure the coast is clear."

Simon summoned a door and was away in a flash.

Lola started picking up plates and cups to bring to the kitchen. Devlin started getting up to help, but Lola shook her head. Through their mind, she told him that she and Jackson might need a moment alone. Devlin stretched out on the couch and closed his eyes.

"I guess my part is done for now," said Jackson as they were loading the dishwasher.

"What's next on the agenda?" asked Lola.

"Considering I only got here yesterday, my whole trip is ahead of me. I'll feel better knowing you are safe," he said.

"I think the worst is over," replied Lola, wiping down the counter.

"So, Tom... is he your boyfriend?" asked Jackson.

"Um, yes, I guess he is," replied Lola, uncomfortable with this line of questioning.

Lola's phone rang, and she jumped. She checked the number, thinking it might be Phyllis calling from Boris' number. But it was Tom's number she saw on the screen.

"It's Tom," she said and headed back to the living room. She nudged Devlin, who immediately opened his eyes. "Tom is calling me, what should I say?" she asked him.

Devlin sat up and replied, "The same thing we told Phyllis."

Lola answered the call. "Hi, Tom... I'm fine, thanks. I'm with Phyllis and Boris," she said, realizing it might not be a good idea to say she had gone home in the middle of the break-in. "I'm sorry if you were worried. But Devlin didn't feel well, and we didn't want to wake anyone in the middle of the night."

Jackson and Devlin were paying close attention to her conversation.

"Look, Tom, we're about to have lunch, can I call you back later?" said Lola.

She agreed to call him back in a few hours. But just before hanging up, Tom said something strange, and she frowned.

"What's wrong?" asked Devlin after she had put her phone back in her pocket.

"Tom said: *I know how much you love being part of the gang and I'm sorry you'll miss the rest of the festivities*," replied Lola.

It was Devlin's and Jackson's turn to frown.

"I guess he doesn't know you that well," ventured Jackson.

"No, everyone at school knows Lola prefers to be by herself or with a very small group of friends," stated Devlin. "Including Tom. I think he was trying to warn you of something. But what?"

"In that case, maybe his uncle prompted him to make the call, and this is Tom's way of saying something is wrong," offered Jackson.

"You may be right. That was an odd thing to say and not at all the way we usually end our phone calls," said Lola, blushing now at the implication that they usually ended their calls with lovey-dovey stuff.

She was saved from further embarrassment when Simon came back.

"All clear on the home front. I checked the surveillance cameras in your office, Jackson. From what I can tell, the intruders left shortly after we did and did not return," said Simon.

Devlin checked his watch. "It's about six a.m. in Virginia and the house is empty. We could go home and rest until Phyllis comes home," he suggested.

"Good plan, I'm so tired I'm about to drop," replied Lola.

They said goodbye to Jackson and wished him a good trip, promising to call or text if anything came up.

As soon as they were home, Lola closed her curtains, stripped down to her underwear, and fell into bed.

She woke up groggily, wondering where she was. Sitting up, her mind cleared, and she remembered the latest in the string of strange and confusing events that were her life. Still, she was glad to be home.

She got up, went to the bathroom, and got a glass of water. She was starving. Padding back to bed, she unplugged her phone from the charger and checked the time. It was one p.m.

She found her robe in the closet, stuffed her feet in a pair of slippers, and made her way down to the kitchen. She was happy to find it empty. Dad and Devlin had either already come and gone or were still asleep. She wondered if her dad had slept in his room now in 2020, or gone back to his own time to check on his Phyllis.

Lola made a pot of coffee, then began the task of making eggs and bacon. She found some blueberry muffins in the freezer and set one to defrost in the microwave. When she was done, she loaded up her feast on a tray and carried it back to her room.

She placed the tray down on her bistro table. She wished she had a balcony as Phyllis did, but she was more than content with her tower.

She padded to the fireplace and found that everything was already set up. All she had to do was light the fire starter log. In minutes she had a roaring fire. She streamed relaxing music to the portable speaker and started eating. This would be her self-care moment of the day since she was unable to get her meditation done.

When she was finished, she brought another cup of coffee up to her loft and checked her email. There was an email from Jane, asking for an update on the 'Tom' situation. Lola wasn't in the mood to respond just then and closed the laptop.

Heading back down, she plopped onto her bed, intending to read. But the combination of breakfast and the warmth in the room had made her sleepy. She kicked off her slippers, shrugged out of her robe, and went back to sleep.

CHAPTER 15
SIMON

SIMON HAD GONE BACK to his time. Once they had come home from the London flat, Simon had asked Devlin to summon the Time Watch so he could travel back and check on Phyllis. He'd been gone since Monday, and Phyllis was sure to worry. At the very least, he had to tell her he might be leaving for a few weeks, should the other Phyllis agree to spend two weeks in Summerset.

For his part, he was dying to go. While they were visiting, it occurred to Simon that the High Elves or Ancient Elves were likely to have advanced medical knowledge and could cure his cancer. He could stop jumping ahead in time and trying so-called miracle cures.

At a minimum, a stay at Summerset was bound to yield vast quantities of interesting knowledge. In addition, it was such a beautiful land he could simply consider it a vacation. There had been precious little time off for him since being diagnosed. He'd been Traveling so much looking for answers about the Keys, the Archives, and the artifacts, then trying to find a cure, Simon wondered how he hadn't collapsed of fatigue until now.

After checking in with Phyllis, he had gone to bed and awoken in mid-afternoon. He took a restorative shower, got dressed, and kissed his sister goodbye. He had dinner plans... with his children.

CHAPTER 16

PHYLLIS

WHEN PHYLLIS GOT HOME, she went straight to the kitchen. She had texted the children to get dinner started earlier. It was already five, so they should be started on it. She had been delayed because she and Boris had decided to take in a Sunday matinee. She knew she'd be home late, but she figured the children might benefit from a few more chores, especially since they'd had to come home due to overindulging at the party. It had actually been Boris' idea, but no one needed to know.

They were in the kitchen, hard at work. Per her instructions, Lola had started defrosting the Brunswick stew Marie had made before leaving. A delicious combination of tomatoes, lima beans, corn, okra, garden-fresh vegetables, and venison.

Devlin was assembling a garden salad and Lola was slicing bread and placing it in a breadbasket. Phyllis put the bakery box she was carrying on the counter. She had stopped at the bakery after the movie to pick up a Napoleon cake. It was a kind of layered crêpe and custard cake. The children would love it.

"Everything seems to be under control here!" she said, hands on her hips, watching her busy bees.

"Phyllis!" exclaimed Lola, dropping her knife and running to her aunt for a hug.

Devlin wiped his hands on the apron he was wearing and also headed towards Phyllis. Since Lola had not yet finished hugging their aunt, Devlin wrapped his arms around both of them and held on tight.

"Darlings, don't get me wrong, I'm lovin' this attention, but I saw you yesterday. Y'all are acting like you haven't seen me in a week!" she chuckled, gently trying to extricate herself. She kissed each of their cheeks and looked them in the eyes. "Did something happen?" she asked, worried now.

"Let's wait for Dad; he's coming to dinner," said Lola.

"Simon! But we haven't seen him in weeks!" shrieked Phyllis.

"It is a long story. A lot has happened since you left us at Tom's yesterday morning," said Devlin.

Phyllis took a deep breath and squared her shoulders. "Aren't they all these days?" she said with a sigh. "Alright, then. Lola darling, put the stew in the oven, it should be warm enough now. Set the timer for six p.m. Devlin, Sugar, go to the cellar and get a bottle, no two bottles of the 2016 Early Mountain Eluvium. I'm going up to shower and change and I suggest you do the same," she said, peering at Lola's pajama bottoms and Devlin's jeans and t-shirt combo. "It's Sunday dinner," she added and danced out of the kitchen.

Back in her room, Phyllis checked her watch and decided she had time for a quick soak. She turned on the water, added some rose petals and Epsom salts to the bath, and went to select an outfit. She'd had her hair done yesterday and it still looked good. She placed a shower cap on it and slipped into the tub.

She and Boris had a lovely weekend, short as it was. Things on that front were going well. *If only they were as easy at home!*

She had mixed feelings about the upcoming fall term. On the one hand, she'd get her life back and could spend more time with Boris when the children headed off to college. On the other, she wished she'd had more time with them over the summer.

The whole business with the new artifacts, and people trying to steal them, was rather bizarre. It had all been so straightforward for Simon and her. You got a Key, and you Traveled. It was all very complicated now.

She forced herself to empty her mind and soak peacefully for the last ten minutes. Enjoying the warm water, she distractedly played with the petals. She already felt better and was looking forward to seeing her brother.

She went down a few minutes before six-thirty to mix some drinks for Simon and her, but he had beaten her to it. He looked so dashing in his gray suit. Of course, it was fifteen years out of style, but the classic cut and the expensive fabric went a long way.

"Oh, Simon! I thought I'd never see you again!" she said rushing towards her older, yet younger, brother like a schoolgirl.

He turned and caught her around the waist before wrapping his arms around her.

"You haven't changed a bit. I saw you only a few hours ago in 2004. Your hair was longer then," he said, kissing her cheek. "I've made your favorite margaritas."

"You read my mind," she said, taking the glass from him. They clinked glasses and went to sit on the sofa.

"What's happened? The children said it was a long story," she said.

"It is, but don't worry, everything is fine," he said, putting a reassuring hand on her knee.

Lola and Devlin walked in, suitably attired, and Phyllis smiled in appreciation.

"If only Mamma and Pappa could be here," said Phyllis, getting misty-eyed. "They would have loved getting to know you."

"Perhaps we can use the Pocket Watch and go back to meet them," said Lola.

"Oh, goodness. I hadn't thought of that," said Phyllis.

"How and when did they die?" asked Devlin.

"I don't recall you ever telling me either. I'm sorry, I never thought to ask," said Lola in apology.

"That's alright, darling. We've had so many other topics to discuss, it never came up," replied Phyllis.

Lola turned to her father. "In your letter to me, you said that all the Evers other than you lived long lives and died from natural causes."

Simon nodded.

"They were both older when Simon and I were born," Phyllis said. "Once Simon was old enough to be Custodian, they toured the world the old-fashioned way. Mamma and Pappa went on an African safari. Not the kind you get from a travel agent; the kind you arrange with a local guide and pay cash for. They wanted the authentic experience," she said.

Simon sighed. "They were in Livingstone, Zambia. Both of them were quite old at this point. They had a long day taking pictures of an elephant herd. When they went back to their hotel, they went to sleep. They never woke up again."

Lola put her hands over her mouth. "You lost them both so suddenly?"

"I think they wanted to leave that way," Phyllis said.

"The doctors at the time said it was heart problems," Simon added. "I agree with Phyllis, though. They left this world together, the way they wanted to."

"My condolences on your loss," said Devlin, looking first to Phyllis, then Simon.

Simon got up and asked, "What can I get you kids to drink?"

Lola asked for a ginger ale and Devlin, who might have taken a beer, asked for the same after one look at Phyllis.

"Phyllis, let me begin by saying I did not overindulge at the party last night. The lie is part of the long story we need to tell you about," said Devlin, exhaling visibly when Phyllis smiled at him in understanding. "Like I told you before, I don't particularly like alcohol, though I enjoy it occasionally."

"Though I'm not too happy about the lie, I'm glad you can drink responsibly, especially when you've got your sister to look after," replied Phyllis a little sternly.

"Quite right," agreed Simon.

"I'm not a child," rebuked Lola.

"Anyway, there was a break-in here last night. We don't think anything was taken; they were looking for the artifacts, which were safely stored in the vault at the attorney's office," started Devlin.

"Someone used my signet ring and imitated my handwriting and sent a note asking the kids to come home," added Simon.

"And when we texted you to confirm, you texted back to come home," concluded Lola.

"Oh sweet Lord, and you walked right into their trap!" cried Phyllis.

"That's where it gets complicated. Dad's been popping in and out of time for a while, and he figured something happened today. So he got here on Monday and has been secretly working with Jackson all week to catch the bad guys," said Lola.

"Jackson?" asked Phyllis.

"More on that later. He's at the London flat and perfectly fine. Don't worry, Phyllis. After he left for his trip, I settled in his office to keep watch on the video feeds. I updated him via text. When I saw him pointing a gun at the children—" said Simon, but Phyllis cut him off.

"Who had a gun?" she shrieked.

"It was Donatelli," replied Devlin. "But we didn't know it at the time, though his Italian accent should have given him away."

"That swine. Did you shoot him with his own gun?" spat Phyllis, incensed.

Lola put a hand to her mouth to keep the nervous giggle from escaping, and Devlin glared at her.

"No one shot anyone. I swooped in and rescued the children just in time. We went back to Jackson's office, then joined him in London. That's when we called you. Because Donatelli had your phone, we were afraid Boris might have been involved, and that'd why we called you with the fabricated story," explained Simon.

Phyllis was in shock. What had this family come to, she thought. Kidnapping, breaking and entering, threats at gunpoint. All in the last three months. She downed her margarita. Simon asked if she wanted another, but she declined. She checked her watch and got up.

"If there's more to this tale, I think we'd best adjourn to the dining room. Lola, will you help me in the kitchen? The boys can set the table," she said and left the room.

CHAPTER 17
PHYLLIS

"WELL, THAT IS QUITE A TALE," said Phyllis, sitting back in her chair and sipping her wine. "And now they want us to spend two weeks with them at Summerset Isle?"

"Yes, but truly it would be like a vacation. You should see it, it's absolutely wonderful," replied Simon.

"Would we have to stay there the whole time or could we come home if we needed to?" she asked.

"I'm sure if there was an emergency, or if you have prior engagements, they would be most accommodating," replied Simon.

"What do you think?" she asked Lola and Devlin.

"I am curious about their land and culture. I believe it is a great opportunity. I am sure we would learn a lot from them," said Devlin.

"Though I agree with Devlin, I was kinda looking forward to spending the next two weeks at home, relaxing before we're due back to school. But with Jackson off on his trip, it's not like I've got many friends waiting for me here. And we'd still be spending time together as a family," said Lola.

"Also, we and our artifacts would be safe from thieves and intruders while at Summerset," added Devlin.

"Yes, that is a good point," said Phyllis, getting up to clear the table.

Lola and Devlin got up and said they would clear the table instead of her.

"Shall we have dessert and coffee in the sitting room?" she asked.

"Yes, good idea. I'll help you with that while the kids clean up in the kitchen."

They made a pot of coffee, sliced the cake, and carried it out on a tray with plates and napkins. The kids would bring coffee and cups when they were done. Simon poured himself and Phyllis each a glass of port, which they should have had after dessert, but Phyllis did not object.

"Is there more you are not telling me?" asked Phyllis.

"Well, I didn't want to get your hopes up, but I have been trying to find a cure," replied Simon.

At Phyllis' hopeful expression, he raised a hand and added, "But I haven't found one. Yet. Only things that make me feel better and seem to be slowing down the process."

Phyllis fell silent. They drank their port.

"Did you go back to visit Mamma and Pappa?" she asked after a moment.

"I did. I even tried to warn them about my cancer, but it happened anyway. I don't think we can change the past. Not big things," he said in apology.

Phyllis nodded "That makes sense. We're not the only ones who have Time Watches. If we could change history by going back in time, it would surely have an impact on the time-space continuum."

"I think that is precisely why the High Elves have invited us to stay with them. We've clearly been acting blindly for years, generations even, and it's time we took responsibility for our family going forward," said Simon.

Devlin and Lola walked into the sitting room with the coffee tray.

"I agree. Especially since I'm the Custodian now and am ultimately responsible for the Evers henceforth," said Devlin.

"Of course, Sugar. You're absolutely right. It's not only a privilege to be invited to Summerset. I believe it may be our duty as well," said Phyllis. "And as your guardian, Lola, what kind of example would I be setting if I didn't do everything in my power to comply with the rules of the Traveling Community, and be informed about any other Community we may be part of."

Everyone got a piece of cake and a cup of coffee. When they had settled back onto the couches, Simon said what was probably on everyone's mind.

"Indeed. We may be part of the Magical Community as well. As far as I know, our parents had no magical ability. Phyllis and I certainly don't have any. But considering one of our ancestors was a powerful sorceress, and the fact that the two of you can communicate through telepathy, it seems there may be more to it than a coincidence."

"From what the High Elves told us, it could be that no one reversed the binding on the twin's powers placed on them after they were born. So the magical ability has lain dormant all these years," suggested Lola.

"But what would have awoken them?" asked Devlin.

"I'm sure that is something the Elves could explain or at least figure out," replied Simon.

"Now that I've gotten used to the whole Traveling thing, and the Time Walking and the World Jumping, I wouldn't mind having magic. The telepathy thing has been very useful so far," said Lola.

"Yes, it has kept us safe," said Devlin.

"Then we are agreed? We'll spend the next two weeks with the Ancient and High Elves?" asked Simon, looking at each of his family members in turn.

"I'm in!" replied Lola.

"Me too," said Devlin.

"As am I," piped in Phyllis.

Simon got up and clapped his hands. "I'll get a pen and paper from the study so we can write our reply to Headmaster Lianon."

"Perhaps we should adjourn to the Library if everyone is finished with dessert," said Phyllis as Simon was leaving the room. "I'll need to consult my daybook to see what needs to be canceled or postponed. And we'll need to make a list of instructions and tasks for Sally and John while we are away."

"Should we not also contact our attorneys to inform them?" asked Devlin.

"Yes, of course," answered Phyllis.

"Simon, get the fire started and we'll join you in a minute," said Phyllis, carrying the remaining cake. Lola got the plates and Devlin brought the coffee tray back to the kitchen.

When they got to the Library, the fire was roaring and Simon was seated in one of the armchairs. Phyllis made for the desk and sat down. Lola went to sit cross-legged on the window seat. Devlin sat by his father.

"I think Devlin should write to the Headmaster. He is head of the family, after all," suggested Simon.

"I am honored, Father. But I believe he is expecting a letter from you in this instance," replied Devlin.

"Since I'm seated at the desk," said Phyllis, "why don't I write it and we can all sign it."

"A diplomatic solution. I like it," said Simon.

"How about I start by asking if we are free to go home if required," said Phyllis. She flipped through her datebook and saw most of her engagements were trivial and could easily be moved. "There's nothing important on the schedule. It's a matter of principle."

It was a short letter. The reply came swiftly. They were guests, not prisoners, and could stay for as long as they were comfortable to do so.

"I'll tell them to expect us after breakfast tomorrow. Is there a time difference there?" asked Phyllis.

"I don't know how time works there. I guess we'll find out," replied Simon.

"Anyhow, Devlin will need to see to the accounts and provide John with instructions. I'll see to Sally," she replied.

"What about me?" asked Lola. "As the spare, shouldn't I be learning how to run the house when you leave or until Devlin marries?"

"How right you are, darling. I think you are mature enough to start learning how to run a house," replied Phyllis.

"Since we're all early birds, perhaps the remaining tasks and list could be done tomorrow morning. Despite the long nap, I'm really quite tired," said Simon.

He hugged each of them good night and took a door back to his own time.

The others made their way to their bedrooms, grateful for an early night.

CHAPTER 18

LOLA

THEY HAD JUST ABOUT COMPLETED their tasks when Sally came into the Library, announcing a visitor. A visitor? This was no time for visitors. Phyllis was about to say as much to Sally when the latter informed her that it was Edward Radcliff, their attorney, and that he had said it was an urgent matter.

"Very well, show him to the sitting room and offer him some refreshments," said Phyllis with a sigh. "What now?"

"Already done, ma'am," said Sally on her way out.

They walked over to the sitting room, greeted Edward, and sat down.

"I'm afraid we're about to leave, Edward. Has something gone wrong?" asked Phyllis.

"Not at all," replied Edward jovially. "I'm to accompany you on your journey."

"What do you mean?" asked Devlin, perplexed.

"I have received an invitation from Headmaster Lianon. He and I have met to discuss my family's involvement with yours," he replied.

Upon seeing Phyllis' concerned face, he quickly added, "I have not divulged any confidential information on the Evers family or your affairs, only on the Radcliffs."

"I see," replied Phyllis, willing Simon to arrive. As if on cue, Simon entered the sitting room, and Phyllis sighed in relief.

"Hello, Edward. It's good to see you again," said Simon, shaking hands with the older gentleman.

"Likewise, Simon. I was just telling your sister and children that I've been invited to Summerset and the Headmaster suggested I travel there with you, so to speak," explained Edward.

"And he has spoken to the Headmaster about our family's long-standing involvement, but not any of the Evers' personal affairs," added Devlin.

"Alright, seems fair," replied Simon.

"However, I wanted to take this opportunity to discuss a related matter with you," said Edward, looking at Devlin.

"As you can see, I'm no longer a young man and will eventually retire. Neither of my children has gone into law and none of the associates at the firm seem likely candidates to take over the Evers Estate and Legacy," he explained.

"Go on," replied Devlin.

"This is the first time there isn't a Radcliff attorney to continue the tradition. And though I am hale and hearty, I will not live forever. I would like to find a worthy successor. Obviously, the firm can continue to work for the Evers family on regular matters, but my concern is for the, ah, irregular matters that seem to be increasing exponentially of late," he explained.

"Do you have a successor in mind?" asked Simon.

"Not anyone specific, but I thought the High Elves could take over. They have very long lifespans and have been involved with Travelers since the very beginning," he replied.

"Indeed," replied Devlin.

"That is the purpose of my visit. So that I can ascertain for myself if they can be trusted. I would also need your approval," he said, addressing Devlin again.

"More decisions!" replied Lola, throwing up her hands.

"I apologize for the added stress, but this is an important, and unprecedented, matter," said Edward.

"Yes, quite. And one that does not have to be taken immediately," replied Phyllis. "Surely we can spend a little time with the High Elves and assess their intentions and worthiness. So far, they've been most gracious and understanding with our family's failings in regards to the Traveling Community."

"That seems fair. They have requested the journals," said Edward.

"What journals?" asked Lola.

"Each Radcliff attorney was tasked with keeping detailed records of their dealings with the Evers over the years. Before a new Radcliff could take over, he was required to read all the journals of his predecessors," explained Edward.

"How many journals are there? Can we read them?" asked Lola.

"There are over a hundred. I don't see why you couldn't read them, though I must warn you most of them are quite boring and hard to decipher. The most interesting ones are from George Radcliff, the first attorney," replied Edward.

"Why?" asked Devlin.

"Because most of his encounters were with Lady Emmeline, the sorceress," he said with a wink.

"Lady Emmeline? She was Lord John Evers' daughter, the one who married Archibald, right?" asked Phyllis

"Correct," replied Edward.

"Wait. If she was a Lady and her father was a Lord, does that mean we're Lords and Ladies as well?" asked Lola, perking up.

"I'm afraid not. Because he did not have a son, Lord Evers' title went to his closest living male relative upon his death," replied Edward.

"Bummer. But that means we have distant relatives that are Lords and Ladies," she exclaimed.

"Very distant," said Phyllis, smiling.

"Do we have any close relatives?" asked Devlin.

"Pappa had a sister, but she never had any children. Any relatives would need to be living descendants of our grandfather's siblings," replied Phyllis.

"We could look into it when we return. I have the family tree at the office. Now, about the journals. I have left them in the automobile. Shall I fetch them and you can read them at the same time as the High Elves do?" asked Edward, getting up.

"Devlin will help you carry them in," said Simon. "Then we should be heading over. Has everyone finished packing?"

"There wasn't much to pack!" replied Lola with a laugh.

In the Headmaster's reply, he had specified that they need only bring items they needed for personal hygiene. Other than the artifacts, they should leave any jewelry, valuables, and electronics at home. Everything they would need, including clothing, would be provided. It was like going on an all-inclusive vacation. Lola wondered if they had pools. She had noticed the air was warm, though not as hot as it was in Virginia in August. Despite all the changes that were happening, she was looking forward to visiting the Ancient Elves' Homeland.

Perhaps the Evers should start keeping journals too. Then she remembered that they did. Each Custodian was expected to record important information in the Archives. But no one ever heard about the sister. Hers would be the first, she decided. Maybe Phyllis could be persuaded to do the same, though Lola doubted it. She loved her aunt to bits, but Phyllis was a little flighty and would probably balk at the idea of recording her thoughts for posterity. Lola had to admit that things had only gotten interesting when she, then Devlin, had arrived in the Family. It would probably be more accurate to say that the trouble had started when Lola arrived. Though Lola had never been a troublemaker, and she often wished she could back to life as a book-worm, she had to admit life was a lot more fun this way. And Lola had a feeling things were about to get even more interesting.

CHAPTER 19

DEVLIN

DEVLIN HAD BEEN GIVEN instructions to arrive directly at the Council Pavilion. When the door opened, they were indeed in front of the building, not in the jungle. They could show Phyllis the jungle later.

The door slid open and they walked in, following the path they had taken with the Headmaster. He was waiting for them in the Atrium with a female High Elf. Seeing the box Devlin carried, he offered to take it. Devlin shot a quick look at Simon for confirmation and relinquished the box.

"I'll take these in and introduce Mr. Radcliff to the Council," he said, "You may remember Aeriearie. She will take you to your dwelling so you may leave your things and get your bearings. You'll join us when you are ready."

He walked away with Edward, who was trying his best to appear non-plussed but failing miserably. He turned back to them and winked.

They followed Aeriearie back through the hall and out the door. Turning right, she led them down a lovely path, close enough to the lake to see it through the trees. Phyllis was taking deep breaths and sniffing the air. "It smells so wonderful here!" she said.

"I believe you are detecting the ozone in the air. I am told this is what it smells like on Earth after it has..." Aeriearie stopped, searching for a word.

"Rained?" supplied Lola.

"Yes, after the rain!" Aeriearie said excitedly.

It was hard to determine her age; she looked a lot like all the other High Elves with long silver hair. But there was an exuberance about her that was endearing. It reminded Devlin of Lola when she was eating dessert. Giddy as a child with a treat.

"Does it never rain here?" asked Devlin.

"Never!" replied Aeriearie.

"But how do things grow?" asked Phyllis in astonishment.

"I've got this one: Magic! I asked the same thing at The Academy," replied Lola with an air of authority.

It never rained at The Academy? He needed to pay closer attention to his surroundings.

Aeriearie laughed. It sounded like birds chirping in a Disney movie. Devlin wondered if she had put a spell on him. He was trying to remember what they had learned about High Elves but he couldn't focus. Her hair was distracting him. Though there was no wind, the silver strands lifted and swayed as she walked ahead of him.

"It's not magic! Summerset is a shallow island; roots access all the water they need from the soil and rain is not required," she answered.

"Fascinating!" replied Devlin dreamily.

Simon, who was walking next to Aeriearie, turned and looked at him. He smiled and nudged Phyllis, who also turned and gave him a wink.

You might want to turn down the admiration a notch, said Lola in his mind.

Aeriearie turned to look down at Lola, her head cocked in confusion.

"Sorry, I was talking to my brother," said Lola, then to Devlin she added, "Sorry..."

Aeriearie turned her amused gaze to Devlin. Mortified, he could feel the heat creeping up his ears. He plastered what he hoped was a neutral smile on his face and emptied his mind the way he had learned in M&M class. She gave a low giggle and whipped around quickly, making her hair fan out and undulate like it was on a roller coaster. She had to have heard his thoughts about her hair and her laugh.

What an idiot! High Elf 101, they can read your thoughts, and even as he thought it, he berated himself for thinking it.

He was saved from further embarrassing thoughts or actions; they had arrived.

The house, or dwelling as Headmaster Lianon had called it, was nearly identical to all the others. It looked like a white modern art deco house but was composed of three tall oblong structures separated only by glass cubes. Those had to be the hallways that led from one to the other. The main 'egg' was the largest. They entered through a huge wooden door that swung in on invisible hinges. Devlin couldn't see a handle, nor had he seen Aeriearie actually push the door open.

It opened onto the main living space, which held white seating options and tables in front of a floor-to-ceiling curved window wall with a view of the lake across the path. They followed Aeriearie to the Elves' version of a kitchen. There was a table with six chairs, all white. The curved back wall held multiple small high windows that let in the light but that humans would be too short to see out of. Below were a counter and cabinets. Devlin did not see any appliances.

Turning left, they went through the first glass passage. Once inside the second 'egg,' they saw two doors.

"These lead to sleeping chambers. They are identical, as are the two in the other structure," she said.

She opened the door to show everyone its contents. There was a large bed, a bedside table, a reading chair, and a wardrobe. She then opened the wardrobe to reveal the clothing and footwear inside. There was no mirror.

"Guest tunics are identical, though they differ from the ones the High Elves wear, which are also different from those of the Ancient Elves. Once you put it on, it will adapt to your shape," she said.

"Like magic?" asked Lola with a smile.

"Yes, like magic!" replied Aeriearie, amused.

She turned and led them back to the main area.

"Would you like me to wait for you or will you be able to find your way back to the Pavilion on your own?" she asked politely.

Simon laughed and told her they would figure it out. She nodded and turned to leave.

"Wait! Um, I didn't see a bathroom. Where do we, um..."

Aeriearie's finger flew to her head, and she replied, "Of course! Follow me."

She turned right, towards the third 'egg.' Opening one of the rooms, Devlin saw they were indeed identical. She walked to the bedside table and touched the glass surface. It lit up instantly.

"That looks like a tablet!" exclaimed Phyllis.

"Yes, it is similar in design and operation. We thought this would be easier for humans to access. Elves would simply intend whatever they require. It is a skill you can learn too. But for now, just tap on the icon you require."

There were eight icons. One was for lights. She tapped it and a sliding scale appeared. She slid it from low to high and the light in the room grew bright accordingly. Next was a glass, which made a glass of water appear on the table. One icon had a bowl. It was grayed out. Aeriearie said it only worked in the kitchen.

The next icon was the toilet. Once tapped, there were two options: toilet with bidet function, and only bidet function. She tapped the toilet image and a box came out of the floor. It had three walls, a door, and a toilet. When she tapped on the icon again, the mini bathroom disappeared into the floor again.

There was a waterfall icon. This led to two options: shower or sink. Tapping on the shower drew a similar box from the floor, but the inside was the shower. There were no knobs and Devlin could not see the showerhead.

Seeing their confusion, Aeriearie explained that once you entered the shower, you would first be sprayed with a cleansing lotion suitable to your species, then water would fall for you to rinse. The water temperature would also be suitable for your species.

"What if I like mine hotter than it is?" asked Lola.

"Simply intend the water to be warmer, or colder for that matter," replied the High Elf.

"That is so cool!" exclaimed Lola.

The shower was sent back and the sink was called up. There was no box, only a sink. This one had the usual knobs.

The next icon was a Venn diagram, each circle a different color. Tapping on this led to multiple options: a cube and a selection of furniture items found around the house.

"I know what this is!" exclaimed Devlin.

Aeriearie motioned for him to tap the controls. He chose the cube. It split into two walls, floor, and ceiling. He chose the floor, then chose a color from the kaleidoscope. The floor immediately turned purple. Phyllis and Lola clapped.

Aeriearie smiled and said, "Humans are very easy to amuse. You should enjoy the next one even more."

She tapped a 'home' icon, which was shaped like an egg. Then she chose the flower icon. It led to a huge selection of pictures. She selected the beach. One of the walls turned into a full-size screen of the beach. Not just an image, but a live feed of a beach.

Devlin walked to it and reached to touch it, but it was only a wall.

"Incredible!" said Simon.

The last icon was a silver swirl, but it was grayed out. "Is that a portal?" asked Devlin.

"Yes, but it only works in the main area," she said.

"Wow!" said Lola.

Aeriearie laughed and added, "Don't get too excited. It has been limited to locations here on the island and is actually not much different from using your Keys to open a door. Which, I should mention, do not work here. You may safely stow them while you are here, as they will prevent you from crossing the portal. You should remove any other jewelry as well."

She tapped the home icon and led them back to the main area.

"If there is anything else, you need only ask," she said.

"How should we communicate with you?" asked Simon.

"Just call out my name. Out loud or in your mind. I will hear you. If I am unavailable, I will send another in my stead," she said as she exited the house.

CHAPTER 20

LOLA

AS SOON AS she saw Aeriearie back on the path, Lola exclaimed, "O.M.G.!" She ran to one of the side tables and tapped on the screen. "Can you believe this place? It's straight out of Architectural Digest but on another level!"

"It is rather extraordinary," replied Phyllis.

With a few more taps, she had changed each sofa to a different color. Next came the walls.

"Darling, I can see that you're having fun, but I thought the white monochrome was rather soothing," said Phyllis, her hand rubbing her forehead. "Perhaps you can decorate your own room when you get the chance."

"She has my sense of color," said Simon proudly.

"I believe they are expecting us," said Devlin, ever the diplomat.

"Quite right," replied Simon. "Kids, you take the left egg, Phyllis and I will take the right one. Let's drop off our things, change into the tunics, and meet back here in, say, twenty minutes?"

Lola and Devlin rushed off to pick a room. As they were identical, there really was no need to rush, but Lola was excited. She was dying to try the shower, but she didn't think she had the time and would feel awkward showing up with wet hair.

She opened the wardrobe and examined the contents more closely. There were two identical tunics, two pairs of shoes, and two sets of what had to be nightgowns. They felt like some kind of linen and were a natural color.

There was room for her backpack, so she stowed it in the wardrobe. After months of wearing her Key around her neck, it felt odd to remove it. She also removed the earrings she had gotten for her birthday from Phyllis and her father's locket. She felt naked, stripped of her personality. These three items were a part of her now; they weren't just jewelry.

She took off her t-shirt and wrapped the jewelry inside, then placed the bundle in her bag's front pocket. She kicked off her Chucks, pulled down her jeans, and wondered about keeping her socks or not. None were provided, so she assumed she wouldn't need them. She was definitely keeping her bra and panties.

Taking one of the tunics, she looked for buttons or a zipper. There were no fasteners, but the head's opening seemed large enough, and the hem was quite large. She pulled the garment over her head and let it float down to the floor. She felt a prickle all over her body; an invisible force was squeezing her. In fact, it was the tunic that was closing in on her and stopped just when it hugged her form but did not mold to her body.

Was it her imagination, or had the neutral beige taken on a subtle purple hue? The hem had also shortened and hovered slightly over her feet. She took a pair of shoes and placed them on the floor. They looked like Mary Janes but were made of some kind of canvas. Maybe everything was made of hemp, she thought. It was a new thing back on Earth; maybe this is where the idea came from.

She slipped in one foot, then the next. Again, there was that squeezing feeling, but it felt good—like a massage. Lifting her skirt to look at her feet, she saw the shoes had molded to her feet. They were comfy too, as was the tunic. She had been afraid it would be scratchy, but it was soft, supple, and felt very breathable. She wished she could see what she looked like. She spun on herself to make the skirt twirl and laughed at her own silliness.

On impulse, she released her hair from the loose bun she wore and shook it out. Taking two strands on either side of her hair parting, she tied them together at the back of her hair as she had seen some of the High Elves wear their hair. There was no way they were going to blend in, seeing as they were a foot shorter than the Elves, but at least she wouldn't stand out too much.

CHAPTER 21
PHYLLIS

IT WAS THE STRANGEST THING. Once Phyllis had donned the tunic and shoes, her hair had started to grow until it reached past her shoulder blades. Curls had unfurled and fell into cascading waves, one or two shades lighter than her normal hair color.

Extending her arms to the side, she saw the tapered sleeves stopped at her wrist, but the color of the fabric now seemed closer to a light peach. This was fortuitous, thought Phyllis, as it would be more flattering.

Despite the absence of mirrors and the identical tunics, it seemed the High Elves were not entirely devoid of vanity. Or perhaps this was their way of accommodating the varying skin tones of humans. High Elves all had that porcelain skin and long silver-blond hair.

When she arrived in the main area, she stopped short, and let a surprised "Oh!" escape her lips. There were two strangers in their house. When they heard her, they turned and to her utter astonishment, it was Simon and Devlin.

Both had long blond hair, silky and straight. Their tunics tapered at the hips and didn't flare out as much as hers did. Devlin's tunic had a light blue hue to his, while Simon's was green. They looked more like brothers than father and son, but they were a handsome pair.

Hands flying to her face, she shook her head in disbelief.

"Lola! You've got to see this. Come quick," she called out.

Lola arrived only moments later and saw her aunt first and smiled. "You look lovely," she said. She followed Phyllis' gaze and stopped abruptly. "You have got to be kidding!"

She burst out laughing and approached the men, walking around them and lifting the strands of their hair, open-mouthed.

"Has my hair grown or changed color? I didn't notice!" she asked, pawing at her dark strands.

"I don't think so, darling. But the hairstyle is very fetching. Would you do my hair the same way?" asked Phyllis.

"You both look like princesses," said Simon.

"While we look like we are headed to COMIC CON," said Devlin stiffly.

"Absolutely not, you look very dashing and every bit as manly as the High Elves," replied Phyllis, smoothing Devlin's hair behind his ear. "Dear God!" she shrieked.

"What's wrong?" asked Devlin in a panic.

Hands flying to her ears, she exclaimed, "Son of a nutcracker!" as she pushed her own hair behind her ears.

They all checked their ears and had very different reactions to finding them to be elongated and pointy. Simon laughed, obviously delighted. Devlin looked at his father, tucked the hair behind his other ear, and shrugged.

"It suits you, son," replied Simon.

Lola dashed to the glass wall, hoping to catch her reflection.

"This is why they don't have mirrors. Please tell me this is temporary!" she said anxiously.

"I certainly hope it's temporary. Can you just imagine me going to my book club looking like this?" said Phyllis, trying to lighten the mood. "However, I do believe we've just found our Halloween costumes for this year!"

"All right, everybody, take a deep breath. We are honored guests in a strange land. We need to accept that things are done differently here and adapt as gracefully as we can. Are we ready to meet the Council?" asked Simon.

They nodded and followed him to the door. As they drew near, Simon put his hand out, thinking there might be a motion sensor, and the door swung in. He took a step back, then halted on the threshold.

"Son of a motherless goat," he said with a chuckle.

"What's happened now?" asked Phyllis.

"Look up," he said, touching the top of the door frame.

Phyllis squinted at him, confused. Lola cocked her head, trying to figure it out.

No one said anything for a minute. Then Devlin said, "We have grown taller!"

"What?" exclaimed Lola.

"The clothing and shoes did not get smaller, we grew bigger! When we arrived, the door was almost twice as tall as us. But look," beamed Devlin, reaching for the door frame like his father.

"How did they do it? I don't remember drinking or eating anything," said Lola.

"This is Summerset darling, not Wonderland!" said Phyllis and laughed.

"But we didn't grow taller when we came yesterday," insisted Lola.

"Good point," said Simon, scratching his chin.

"Perhaps when we removed our Keys and other metal adornments, we became susceptible to the planet's gravitational forces," suggested Devlin.

"You're such a nerd. Why didn't I think of that?" replied Lola.

"Okay, time to go. And just a heads up, I think my beard is about to grow out. Is your face itching, Devlin?" Simon asked.

"No, not at all," he replied, passing a hand over his cheek.

"Maybe it comes with age," said Simon, clapping him on the back. "Come on."

CHAPTER 22

EDWARD

"ALDERAN WORKS at the Knowledge Center. When we acquire texts from other lands, they are cataloged, restored as needed, processed, and placed in the Knowledge Center. There are three processing teams. He is on the first team. They are speed readers who can absorb large quantities of data and share it with others. They share the content with the second team, the translators. They translate the data into our language, then into every other language that we have acquired. Once they have completed this task, the third team takes over. They are responsible for uploading the information to our Knowledge bank, accessible to the collective. They also index it so it can be parceled into smaller units for easier absorption," explained Saruir.

Edward cocked his head in confusion. "I apologize, but are you not speaking English at present?" he asked.

"Yes, we are. As Council Leader, I must be fluent in most languages. As is Headmaster Lianon. However, Alderan absorbed parcels of British and American English before the meeting," explained the Leader.

"Absorbed. It sounds like he ingested it," replied Edward, laughing.

"That is not far from the truth. After absorbing knowledge, one always feels full," replied Alderan.

"Extraordinary. And how long will it take you to read all of these journals?" asked Edward.

Alderan took the bundle of George Radcliff's journals and untied the ribbon that bound them together. Taking the first one, he flipped through it, then checked if the others were similar.

"This group should take me about fifteen minutes. I would estimate no more than an hour for the lot of them. May I take them to my office?" he asked Edward.

"Yes, of course," replied Edward, amazed.

He gently put the journals back in the box and left the room.

Simon and his family had not yet returned from settling into their dwelling. Edward continued to discuss his lack of a successor with the Headmaster and the Council Leader.

"We have competent associates, one of which has recently been made a partner in the firm. He is more than capable of taking care of the Evers' regular affairs. Though this will still require some preparatory steps since some of the terms in their legacy documents are odd, often referring to magical aspects," said Edward.

"Lianon and I have discussed the matter following his conversation with you. We understand the position you are in, and your desire to retire in peace. Would you consider staying on as an advisor, solely for the Evers?" asked Saruir.

"I would. My father did the same, but as he ages, I'm afraid his memory cannot be relied upon. It will be the same for me, eventually," replied Edward, sadly.

"I'm thinking of a temporary situation. Here is what I propose. I believe you employ legal assistants who are not attorneys but are bound by the same confidentiality terms, correct?" asked Saruir.

"Yes, that is correct. We have legal assistants and paralegals. They have access to all of our files, except the Evers'. Those we handle personally," explained Edward.

"Since you are retiring soon, and because the Evers are your most important client file, it would not be unheard of to hire such an assistant at this time," asked Lianon.

"It would be logical, but our contract with the Evers stipulates that only a Radcliff attorney may be involved," stated Edward.

"Here is what I propose. Summerset could supply you with an assistant. The High Elf would appear human, the way Lianon did when he visited you. You could draft a new contract with the Evers to allow this, with a stipulation that the assistant will be replaced every forty years or so by a successor of his own choosing. It would be one of our speed readers—possibly Alderan, as he would welcome the challenge and opportunity," suggested Saruir.

"But after I'm gone, an attorney will be required," objected Edward.

"While he is with you, Alderan will complete his studies to become a certified attorney. With his abilities, that would be accomplished rather quickly, though I understand certain formalities would need to be observed."

"It would normally take at least seven years to obtain a *Juris Doctor*, usually required to register for the Bar Examination. However, the state of Virginia is one of four states where it is still possible to *Read Law*. There is a program by which a person may apprentice with an attorney for three years before taking the Bar Exam," replied Edward.

"Splendid," exclaimed Lianon. "If Alderan is willing, he could take whichever avenue would be the swiftest so that you may retire as soon as possible. Does that sound amenable to you?"

"It sounds perfect," said Edward, who sighed in relief. "Assuming the Evers are in agreement, of course."

"Of course," replied Saruir.

Edward sat back in his chair and exhaled, relaxing for the first time since he had arrived in this strange land. He had recognized Headmaster Lianon, though it had been a bit of a shock seeing him in his true form. The man, or rather High Elf, had appeared slightly older than him when they met in his offices. Now, he looked timeless, as did the Leader Saruir. He had been told that Saruir was an Ancient Elf, but other than wearing slightly different attire, Edward could not see much of a difference between the two species. What he did see, was that he looked older than everyone in Summerset, though they were all hundreds of years older than he. Perhaps they could offer some tips or even a tonic that would help him age more gracefully in the coming years. Though he had to admit he was excited at the prospect of having an apprentice. What fun that would be, molding him into the best attorney he could be, passing on his wisdom the way they did in centuries past.

He was roused from his musings when the door opened and in came four High Elves. Edward wondered who they were. When one of them gave him a small wave, he sat up straighter and stared open-mouthed at the Evers family.

"Dear God, is that what I look like as well?" he exclaimed, looking at Saruir and Lianon in horror.

"No, I'm afraid you still look like your human self," replied Lianon with a chuckle. "Non-magical humans do not change forms when visiting Summerset. However, those with magical abilities will take on an Elf-like form while they are here, provided they remove all metal from their person. Metals, specifically iron, are incompatible with High Elf physiology."

Edward breathed another sigh of relief and rose to greet the newcomers.

"Don't you look the vision," said Edward, taking Phyllis' hand and depositing a kiss on it.

Phyllis giggled like a schoolgirl.

"Indeed," replied Lianon, taking her arm and showing her to a seat at the table.

"Miss Lola, how lovely you look," said Edward with a small bow.

Lola blushed and thanked him. Alderan had just entered the room behind them.

"May I escort you to the table, Miss?" he asked in flawless English.

"Um, yes, thank you, Alderan," replied Lola, taking his arm and looking back at Devlin.

Edward shook hands with Simon and Devlin. "You both look very dashing," he said with a chuckle, and they all took their seats.

CHAPTER 23

SIMON

WITHIN A SHORT AMOUNT OF TIME, the Council Leaders had joined them to draft a plan of action. Simon would stay with Saruir, Headmaster Lianon, Edward, and the new High Elf named Alderan. Phyllis would go with Rumena for a crash course in all things related to Travelers and their artifacts. Lola and Devlin would go with Aeriearie to the Science Pavilion to assess their magical abilities.

As the remaining Council members left to continue with the investigation of the suspects, Saruir approached Simon and asked to have a private word with him. They moved away from the group.

"Am I correct in assuming you would like to remain an active part of your children's lives?" asked the Council Leader.

"Well, yes, of course, I would like to remain in their lives. But, as I'm sure you are aware, I am from the past, and Traveling on borrowed time due to illness," replied Simon.

"I believe we may be of mutual assistance," he said cryptically.

"What do you mean?" replied Simon, unable to keep the hope out of his voice.

"There is no illness among our people, nor can illness exist in our world. At the moment, you are in optimal health and will remain so for as long as you stay in Summerset," he said.

"I see," said Simon, dejectedly. "But when I go back to Earth, I'll still have cancer."

"If you stay here long enough, you will eventually be immune to Earthbound illnesses," he said cheerfully.

"How long is long enough?" he asked, expecting him to say a century or two.

"If you stayed for three or four months, you'd be well on your way to building an immunity," he said. "Then you could go home and live without worry of the cancer progressing."

"But I would need to return to Summerset eventually, right?" he asked.

"Correct," replied Saruir.

"Would I stay like this?" asked Simon, pointing at himself.

Saruir laughed. "No, as soon as you retrieve your Key, you will revert back to your human form."

Well, that confirms Devlin's theory, he thought.

"And what would I do here?" he asked.

"That is where we may be of mutual assistance! You see, the Academy needs a part-time visual arts teacher for the winter term. Because the Academy is in a world of its own, your illness will not progress while you are there. Instead of living on campus with the other staff members, you would live here in Summerset and commute via a portal. You'll need to discuss the details with Lianon."

"Does the Headmaster know about this?" asked Simon.

"It was his suggestion," explained Saruir.

"Would I look like a High Elf while at The Academy?" asked Simon.

"For the first four months, it would be better if you did. And should you stay on at The Academy for the winter term, it would be confusing for the students were you to change back into a human," remarked Saruir.

"Yes, of course. I would consider it an honor more than a burden," said Simon, relaxing for the first time in months.

"As well you should, since you will become an honorary High Elf!" replied Saruir with a wink.

He was making a joke, Simon thought, and smiled at the Council Leader.

"I accept your proposition," said Simon, happier than he had been in a long while.

"You have not heard the terms," protested Saruir.

"All right, let's hear them," said Simon, bracing himself.

"You may no longer use the Time Watch or the Sphere. They must be relinquished to the children," he started.

"Agreed. But when I do go back to Earth, when will I go back? To my own time or that of the children?" he asked.

"Your time on Earth will be limited to visits to the Evers home and Estate, in the present time only. As you are considered to be deceased, it would be unwise to wander," replied Saruir.

"But don't I need to go back and, well, die?" said Simon, squirming at the thought of his own demise.

The experience of dying had not yet happened to him, as he was traveling in time before he died. But he knew that in the timeline, he had in fact died of cancer in 2005.

"We can fix the blip in the timeline that would have you disappear before your own death," said Saruir, waving this off.

"Okay. One day, I'll want to know how you did that, but not today," said Simon, shaking his head. "There is something else…"

Saruir shook his head, as though he knew what Simon was going to say. "I'm afraid we cannot bring Elaine Harris through time. As a Time Traveler and World Jumper, this opportunity is unique to you."

Simon's shoulders slumped. "I needed to know all the same. But if I am going to be here for my children, I can't feel guilty that their mothers can't, too."

"Agreed. The next condition, beyond staying here for four months, is that you can only leave for four weeks at a time before you must return. Should you accept the position at the Academy, that is the time off between semesters anyhow."

"Seems like plenty of time to spend with my family," he replied.

"Every time you go to Earth, you will age more rapidly," warned Saruir.

"Considering I'm fifteen years younger than I should be, I don't see that as a problem," responded Simon with a chuckle.

"For every week on Earth, you will age one year or eight years per annum," stated Saruir.

"I'll have to do the math. In my time, I was thirty-three, though had I lived I would be forty-eight. In two years, I'll have caught up to my present age. Another two years puts me at fifty-five. I'll be eighty by the time the kids graduate from the Academy. If I want to live longer, I may need to reduce the number of weeks I spend on Earth," said Simon.

"Indeed. But remember, you will see your children at school, and your sister can visit every Sunday," said Saruir, in a milder tone.

"Still worth it, anything else?" he asked.

"When I said your time on Earth would be limited to the Evers mansion and Estate, I was also implying that you would no longer Travel," said Saruir, looking intently at Simon.

"Yes, I got that part. Every day that I get to spend with my children and my sister is a gift and you are offering me years and years. I cannot refuse," said Simon, clasping his hands together in front of him in peaceful surrender.

"Very well. I'll let Lianon know of your acceptance, and we'll meet later this week to make the arrangements. Would you care to discuss this with your family, first?" he asked before heading back to the meeting table where the others were pouring over the journals.

"No, I know they will agree with me and will be overjoyed at the opportunity," said Simon, grinning from ear to ear as he joined the others.

CHAPTER 24

DEVLIN

GETTING their magical abilities assessed was all very exciting, if a little frightening. Lola and Devlin were asked to step onto small round platforms. Once positioned, they were told to relax and breathe normally before being encased in glass cylinders. Large disks attached to a robotic arm rose up from the floor and did a 360-degree scan all the way to their head, where it stayed a little longer before gliding back down. The cylinders lifted, and they were told to step off the platform. The entire operation took less than five minutes.

They were invited to sit at a table. At a nearby console, a High Elf introduced as Celenious was looking over their scans. He sent them to the screen on the wall so they could all study them. There were three scans: Lola's, Devlin's, and one from a 'control' human.

Devlin could see differences between them and the control human. For one thing, everything was brighter on their scans.

"If we are in High Elf-like bodies, how can the scan be accurate?" asked Devlin, wondering if perhaps that explained the differences.

"The control human was also in a High Elf body at the time of the scan," replied Aeriearie. "Celenious, can you pull up my scan to compare?" she asked the High Elf at the console.

It appeared first on his screen, then he sent it to the larger one they were looking at.

If their scans had been bright, hers was positively glowing in comparison. Each of her systems showed in bright silver or gold, whereas Lola's and Devlin's were bold, dark colors. The control human's systems were the same colors as theirs, but paler and uneven in some areas.

"Let's start with the sympathetic and parasympathetic systems. Both of yours look healthy and strong; flowing easily. That is in part because of your age and, I would guess, general healthy lifestyles. Our control human has blockages here, and here," he said, pointing to areas on the scan.

Lola and Devlin nodded. They had studied some of this in biology, but Devlin was waiting for the great reveal. Celenious spoke at length about their circulatory systems and their meridians. Devlin was starting to lose focus when Celenious finally zoomed in on their brains. Things were getting interesting.

There were clear differences in all four scans. Aeriearie's scan showed high activity in all areas. The neocortex was sizeably larger than all three other brains on display. Zooming in further revealed millions upon millions of connections in all parts of her brain. The image reminded Devlin of that scene in the last *Twilight* movie where everything was coated in silver. Aeriearie's brain, compared to the control human's, looked like something out of a sci-fi movie where a scientist took a monkey and turned it into a smart chess player or a genius mathematician.

Lola's and Devlin's brains had similarities and differences. Both had very active right hemispheres. This was where most of the extrasensory abilities originated from. However, each of them had different parts of the brain that contained more connections due to the fact that they used those sections more often.

Celenious pulled up another brain scan and compared it to Aeriearie's. It too had a larger neocortex and a large number of silvery connections but was shaped differently from a human brain.

"Is that a dolphin brain?" asked Devlin, remembering he had watched a documentary on cetacean intelligence.

"Correct!" exclaimed Celenious, beaming at Devlin like he was a star pupil.

Devlin had no idea how old Celenious was, but he still enjoyed the praise. "Cetaceans include whales, porpoises, and dolphins, and while all are considered intelligent, dolphins' abilities appear to outclass them all," he added.

"Dolphins share our abilities to communicate with each other, as well as share knowledge and echolocation," explained Celenious, who then expanded on the topic until he noticed that Lola was getting antsy.

Devlin could also see she needed to move.

Aeriearie suggested they proceed with individual testing and that perhaps Devlin and Celenious continue their discussion on their own.

Devlin was pleased, and Lola looked momentarily relieved. Then Devlin saw a worried look creep into her face.

What is wrong? he asked in his mind.

What kind of tests do you think they're going to do? she replied.

I am assuming non-invasive cognitive testing, he replied.

But why do we have to be separated? she asked.

Surely to test our telepathic abilities, he answered. *Do not worry, Lola.*

She nodded and left with Aeriearie.

CHAPTER 25
PHYLLIS

PHYLLIS NEVER WANTED TO LEAVE. When Lola had jokingly said their stay here would be like going to an all-inclusive resort, she had no idea how prophetic that would turn out to be.

Upon leaving the Council Pavilion, Rumena had led her to the Knowledge Center. Phyllis had assumed that was an elegant word for a library. The building was similar in design to the one they had just left, and only a short walk away, on a path leading away from the lake this time.

Once inside, Phyllis was astonished to find it was a hive of activity. There were multiple meeting rooms where groups of High or Ancient Elves were discussing issues, and from the animated expressions on faces, she could see through the glass partitions, the topics seemed very interesting.

There were two large classrooms. Ancient Elves were instructing High Elves who appeared to be hanging on their every word.

In the middle of the room, there were tables and chairs. Some were occupied by those reading scrolls or books. While others were filled with Elves who had their hands clasped around white cubes, their eyes closed, eyelids fluttering rapidly. Perhaps it was a form of power meditation. She would have to ask Rumena, but for now, she was content to observe.

They headed towards the far end of the room where three tall columns rose to the ceiling. Each had a symbol Phyllis did not recognize on it. Rumena chose the middle column and stopped in front of it. She closed her eyes and lifted a hand. It hovered close to the column but did not connect with the surface. Within seconds, an invisible drawer slid out soundlessly. A white cube was nestled inside. Rumena picked it up and motioned for Phyllis to follow her back to one of the meeting rooms.

"Normally, we would sit at one of the tables. But as we may need to discuss a few things, it's best we take a room. I believe this is a common practice in your libraries as well. Correct?" she asked.

Phyllis nodded and followed Rumena into a room and sat down.

"There are three ways of acquiring knowledge in Summerset. The first is instant and happens telepathically through intent. This is useful for everyday tasks, or with knowledge you do not need to retain but may require at a moment's notice," explained the High Elf.

"Like Google," replied Phyllis.

Rumena was obviously familiar with Earth culture and laughed. "Yes, but much faster and no device is required!" she exclaimed.

"That would be very useful. Especially since as we age, we become forgetful," said Phyllis with a sigh.

"Even by human standards, you are not old. How many years do you have?" asked Rumena, assessing her new friend.

"I am forty-six years old," replied Phyllis.

"That's an infant here! I'm 124 years old," admitted Rumena proudly.

"And yet you don't look a day over forty," replied Phyllis.

"Enough of that, though I admit this human custom of giving compliments is amusing," she stated. "The second method of acquiring knowledge is the traditional way, through reading texts and listening to lectures. As old as our civilization is, we cannot circumvent it since it is still the way many worlds, including Earth, transmit knowledge."

"That's what they are doing in the large rooms over there. Correct?" asked Phyllis, pointing at the classrooms.

"Yes, today the lectures are offered by Ancient Elves. But sometimes we have lecturers from other worlds. That is most elevating!" said Rumena, eyes shining.

"And the meeting rooms?" asked Phyllis.

"As you would imagine. Some are students collaborating on a project, others are debating topics, while some are working on new policies or initiatives," said Rumena.

"Alright, what's the third way?" asked Phyllis

"Learning through osmosis," announced the High Elf.

Phyllis blinked.

Rumena placed the cube in front of Phyllis. "Our knowledge can be delivered by touch to any being of any world. I could simply take your hand and send it to you. However, not all beings have the capacity to process all that information in one go. Most of them don't require it. The only time it would be required is if I were the last being in my world and had to transfer the knowledge quickly so it wasn't lost," said Rumena seriously.

Phyllis maintained her famous southern composure and nodded for her companion to continue.

"We have indexed our knowledge and divided it into more manageable parcels, tailored to the being's capacities and area of interest. This cube contains the knowledge a Traveler would acquire during their first Summer Program at The Academy," she explained.

"And I just place my hands around the cube and close my eyes?" asked Phyllis.

"Correct, it will take less than a minute," said Rumena.

"Will it be... uncomfortable?" asked Phyllis.

"Your pulse might be elevated, and some people have reported feeling dizzy, but only for a moment. This is the smallest parcel I could give you. After this one, we'll decide if you want to stop, continue at this rate, or increase the dose, so to speak," she explained.

Phyllis took a deep breath and placed her hands on the table on either side of the cube.

When she was ready, she cased the cube in both hands and closed her eyes. Though Rumena had said it would take less than a minute, to Phyllis the experience felt like the full two weeks. The cube didn't only contain information, it contained feelings, impressions, and moment-by-moment experiences like eating in the Dining Room, sleeping in the dorm, taking notes, having fun at the BBQ, learning to meditate, and so on. It was like they had recorded every aspect of every year one student's experience, mashed it up, and uploaded it to Phyllis' memory.

When she opened her eyes, she didn't feel dizzy. She felt giddy, tired, and... alive!

"Holy Moly!" exclaimed Phyllis, letting go of the cube and standing up. She was full of energy now.

"May I have another?" she said, feeling like an addict.

Rumena chuckled and rose to return the cube and retrieve another.

"One more, then we're going to the spa," she said, stepping out of the room.

And here she was, not at a spa, but at the Wellness Center. She'd had a long, hot shower. That in itself had been an experience because she hadn't realized you had to tell the shower to begin. In truth, you were meant to *intend* the shower to start and then stop. But it seemed that despite years of meditation, and a magical ancestry, this was not a skill she possessed.

After her shower, she had donned a robe and joined Rumena in the great room. From there, she could choose from various treatments, similar to those you would find in a spa on Earth, except all the products were sourced from the island. Not creams and potions made from ingredients, but actual mud from the waterfall, mineral water from a cave, fruit nectar, and flower petals.

This was her reward for completing the first two installments of the Summer Program. She felt fortunate—Lola and Devlin had to actually cram five years' worth of information into two weeks, without the experience. *They must have had so many questions!* She was happy now she hadn't pestered Rumena with endless questions on her way to the Knowledge Center, for all had been answered.

This is the good life. I wonder why I don't do more of this at home.

The High Elves looked fantastic and enjoyed long, happy, and healthy lives. And this was apparently part of their routine. She would add more self-care activities to her own—beyond yoga, meditation, and getting her hair and nails done.

After the mud bath, she showered and was treated to a full body scrub and then a massage. She couldn't wait to hear what the others had done with their day.

CHAPTER 26

LOLA

ONCE THEIR SCANS had been analyzed, Lola left with Aeriearie, while Devlin remained in the lab with the other scientist for some one-on-one testing. Lola was reluctant to leave, as she felt safer with Devlin. But Aeriearie insisted they should be tested separately to have accurate readings.

They didn't go far, and Lola felt stupid for wanting to stay with her brother. The testing rooms were just off the main lab. She saw Devlin and his tester head further down the hall. Worst-case scenario, she could just call him telepathically, though Aeriearie would surely hear.

"How do I purposefully block my thoughts from you?" she asked.

"I'll show you when the tests are complete, as hearing thoughts will be required during our tests," answered the High Elf.

The first part of the test seemed like a standard psychological assessment. The questions and images to interpret were similar to an assessment Lola had to take following the death of her mother. The grief counselor at school had been worried about depression and anxiety, but found that Lola was coping well and was fit to continue her studies until the end of the school year.

The next part was a fine and gross motor and coordination assessment, followed by visual and auditory acuity tests. She had a good idea of the results of those as well. She had great fine motor skills, terrible gross motor ones, perfect vision, and excellent hearing.

The last set of tests were the most interesting—they were to measure her extra-sensory perception such as telepathy, precognition, telekinesis, clairvoyance, and astral projection.

She already knew she had some telepathic abilities, but she was surprised to know she also had clairvoyant abilities. Aeriearie made her guess images on cards that were hidden from her view. The images were a combination of colors, shapes, and dimensions that she could not randomly guess with a set probability of accuracy, like if they were only colors or shapes. Her accuracy rate was ninety percent, and Aeriearie said she could improve to the point of being 100% correct consistently. The precognition was hard to measure because it seemed like logic and deduction to her. Aeriearie would tell her a story and ask what came next. Apparently, she was quite good at it, but there was always room for improvement.

She had no natural ability for telekinesis, but Aeriearie said that part of the brain showed a predisposition and that they would work on it during the week. The final test was astral projection or out-of-body experience. She knew Phyllis could do it, as they had found out from the time she was kidnapped, so she should be able to do it too. Aeriearie had her close her eyes and focus on her breathing for a little while to achieve a meditative state. Then she led her through a guided meditation to a place that was unknown to her, and would ask her to describe what she saw. This was followed by another and then another place. She brought Lola back to her current position but asked her to remain in the meditative state. Some time elapsed before she asked Lola to go back to the second place, which was the top of a hill. That was her favorite, and the view was spectacular. She recognized it as the valley in Summerset. She could see the lake, the Pavilions, the path, the houses, and the jungle or forest beyond. It was truly breathtaking. She heard a noise behind her and turned to investigate. It was Aeriearie! She joined Lola near the edge of the cliff and looked out at her land, a serene smile on her face.

"I am told there are places of equal beauty on Earth," she said.

"Yes, there are. But the air here is sweeter, and the energy is stronger," replied Lola.

"Let's sit for a while," suggested Aeriearie, and they sat cross-legged on a nearby rock.

There was no conversation for at least fifteen minutes. They were both in silent contemplation, content to simply enjoy the moment, the view, the sounds, the smells, and the feel of the air. Lola took deep breaths, exhaling slowly. The more she took, the better she felt until she felt so giddy, she wondered if the air was addictive.

It's not, replied Aeriearie in her mind. *What you're feeling is a state of bliss or pure positive energy. A connection to all that is.*

Is that how you feel all the time? Lola asked.

Most of the time. But sometimes it's not practical to be in a state of bliss, replied Aeriearie.

"What do you mean?" asked Lola, slipping out of her thoughts.

"Let me show you," said her companion.

Instead of words or thoughts, Aeriearie sent images and experiences to Lola. They were so vivid that Lola was transported to the time and place that Aeriearie was describing. She was in a room with other High Elves, debating a topic with great animation. She looked around for her new friend, but could not see her. She understood why when one of the High Elves said, "What do you propose, Aeriearie?"

She was not only seeing through Aeriearie's eyes, she was Aeriearie, and had access to her feelings, knowledge, and memories. She felt eager, curious, and determined. She heard herself say, "I believe we ought to create a permanent portal with Earth, so humans can come and learn from us. It would be more efficient than having multiple High Elves disguised as humans trying to influence them. If the humans came here to learn, they would go back and share their experience with others and it would feel more authentic to those they told because it would be part of their human experience and thus be more relatable."

There was equal agreement and disagreement from her fellow High Elves. Lola felt herself lift up and drop into the mind of one of the

High Elves who had disagreed. She felt his acceptance of Aeriearie's suggestion—there was no judgment, only gratitude for the new point of view. He felt calm, satisfied, yet passionate.

Lola, as him, replied, "You make a valid point. We cannot offer a relatable point of view to humans based solely on the fact that we look like them while on Earth. And I agree that humans would reap tremendous benefits from such an internship in Summerset. However, who are we to assert our way of thinking? By providing knowledge to select individuals, we are in fact creating prophets who will return to Earth to convert as many people as possible, implying that the way they think and act is inferior or inadequate. Whereas when we visit, we are planting seeds of a different, not better or worse, way of being."

Again, everyone voiced their opinions. Familiar with the feeling now, Lola rose out of this High Elf and into another. This was so much fun. She wished all debates were this civilized.

"I believe you may both be right. On the one hand, the beings that chose Earth as their home were well aware of the density of the planet and accepted the range of experiences they would have access to. Even those that may be deemed negative by the human mind. However, it is their collective intention to rise out of the current dimension they are in. A growing number of humans agree they have stayed too long in the third dimension and are actively seeking ways to evolve or ascend. There are other beings there, assisting them. There are also beings intent on keeping them locked into their victim roles. Magic has been absent from the Earth for too long. I believe it must be restored, and we have the ability to point them in the right direction. Is it not our responsibility to assist when assistance is clearly requested? To show the way to those who seek the path? To be a light, or a beacon, that humans emulate instead of following blindly? Should they not be empowered instead of being converted?"

This High Elf felt powerful, engaged, and, well, high. It was the only word Lola could find for the feeling. It wasn't the same giddiness she had felt on the hill; there was a subtle difference. It called to action instead of reflection. But both were felt in her heart chakra.

She felt a hand on her shoulder. "Come back to the lab."

Instantly she was back in the lab, her feet heavy on the ground, her buttocks and back firmly set in the chair. She opened her eyes and smiled at Aeriearie.

"That was amazing!" she said.

"Before you allow yourself to be influenced by unnecessarily human emotions, can you describe the difference between bliss and power?" she asked. "You were almost there a minute ago, but I wanted to see if you could hold on to the feeling."

Lola closed her eyes and called up the giddy feeling. She felt it near her heart. It radiated within her body, but also outside her body, like pulsing waves. It felt like love, unconditional love, and made her want to hug everyone.

Good, keep going, thought Aeriearie.

She called up the feeling of power. It also came from the heart, but it expanded throughout her chest, upwards and outwards like an inverted triangle. She felt the surge of energy rise to her throat chakra willing her to speak her truth. It then moved up to the third eye, beaming out so others could see her vision and up through her crown chakra where she felt a column of pure silver light shoot straight up to the heavens and bounce back to her, like the high striker game at carnivals. The beam came down much stronger, like a deluge, and kept going past the heart, out through her arms, down her spine, and down through her legs, exiting through her feet, shooting out from there and into the ground. She felt invincible, grounded, and tall.

Well done, Lola, sent Aeriearie. *You can open your eyes now.*

Lola opened her eyes and stood up. She needed to move, to stretch, to go do something.

"If I felt like that back at home, I'd be unstoppable," she said, excited.

"You *can* feel like that back at home. You just need to call up the feeling. It might take a little more effort, but you'll get there," assured Aeriearie.

"Fantastic!" exclaimed Lola. "How were you able to share the other two High Elves' point of view with me?"

"Because they shared them with me. We always share with each other. That is why we don't actually need to talk because we always know what the other is feeling and thinking," she replied.

"Then why do you debate?" asked Lola.

"Because it's fun and we can maintain our language skills. Earth is not the only world where talking is the norm," she replied.

Lola nodded. She was still standing, feeling super grounded but needing to expend some of her energy.

Aeriearie nodded and rose from her chair. "I think that's enough for today," she said. "What would you like to do?"

"What can we do?" asked Lola.

"Anything you want," replied the High Elf.

"I'd really like to hike up the hill and go back to that spot," replied Lola. "Would that take too long?"

"You may have noticed the absence of clocks or watches here. Time is an Earthly concept," explained Aeriearie.

"But how do you organize meetings? How do you know it's time for lunch?" asked Lola.

"Let me explain it on the way," she said and opened the door. They went out into the hall and walked toward the room Devlin was in. The door was open and it was empty.

"Perhaps they decided to go outside, too," suggested Lola.

"Perhaps," she replied with an amused smile.

"You know where they are, right?" asked Lola.

"I know where every High Elf and Ancient Elf is at all times, and I know what they are doing, and thinking," was her response.

"That sounds creepy and intrusive," laughed Lola, shuddering slightly.

"I can see why you would think that, but things are different here. Also, if you wanted to know where your brother was, you could simply ask him," replied Aeriearie.

Lola thought of this and gave her head a smack. Of course. She could always communicate with Devlin, anywhere, anytime. But she was happy not to know what he was thinking and feeling all the time.

"I get your point. Just because I have access to the information, doesn't mean I need to link to it 24/7," she said.

"Correct," said Aeriearie, clapping her hands in approval. "So, where is he?"

"I don't need to know, let's go on our hike," she said finally.

CHAPTER 27

SIMON

AT THE END of the day, everyone reconvened in the Council room. Once they were all seated, Saruir asked Alderan to present his report. He touched the timeline on the screen and swiped it in the direction of the big screen where it landed for all to see. It started with Emmeline's birth and ended with Devlin becoming Custodian. He gave them an overview of the events, which included the birth and death of both Evers and Radcliffs, major land or property sales and purchases, use of the Time Watch and/or Sphere, as well as surges of magical ability. Magical abilities stopped with the birth of Emmeline and Archibald's twins and only resumed when Lola and Devlin met. Simon and Phyllis' grandparents had the most property transactions and had bought six homes worldwide. Simon had been the sole user of the Time Watch thus far.

Alderan then presented an updated version of their family tree. This one included the generation before Emmeline and Archibald, since the family had asked about possible living relatives.

Emmeline's mother had also died in childbirth, and Emmeline was her only surviving child. However, Emmeline's mother, Rose Analise Harding, had a sister named Petunia Eva. She married Sir Anthony

O'Callahan, a visiting Irish aristocrat. He took her back to his estate in the Wicklow Mountains, just outside of Dublin. They had three sons: Brady, Conor, and Ian. The eldest died of influenza. Ian became a clergyman and Conor became the heir. He married and had identical twin sons: Kieran and Larkin. The eldest inherited the Estate, as was the custom, but it created a rift between the brothers. Seeking peace, Kieran gave his brother one of the family estates in county Cork, so he could live comfortably and find a good match while being far enough away that the brothers would not run into one another and could live their lives independently. Larkin agreed and dropped the O' from his name. He became Larkin Callahan.

At this point in the tale, Lola raised her hand. Alderan seemed unfamiliar with this practice and looked to Lianon who nodded for Lola to speak.

"I'm sorry to interrupt, but I think I know where you're going with this. I think, if you scroll down to Larkin's living descendants, you will find Tom and Tabitha Callahan. Am I correct?" asked Lola, with a pained expression.

Phyllis gasped and Devlin hung his head. The Headmaster said, "Oh dear."

"How did you know?" asked Alderan, bemused.

"We go to school with Tom. He is the nephew of Aidan Callahan, one of the suspects," explained Lola.

"I see, that makes you distant cousins and certainly provides a motive for recent events."

Simon could see that Lola was distressed. This had to be the boyfriend!

"Lola, honey, that makes you very, very, very distant cousins. Since Evers always had their children young, we are around fourteen generations from our last common ancestor on our side. Were you and Tom to marry, it would not have led to any birth defects, the kinship is too weak," he said reassuringly.

Lola blushed, and he realized he'd made a mistake in speaking about this in front of everyone. But it was too late now.

"That's not it. This information makes it less likely that Tom was an innocent bystander to his uncle's plans. Especially with the weird phone call," said Lola.

"All right, we seem to have mismatched information. The easiest way to resolve this is to join hands and open your minds," said Saruir, clasping hands with the people on either side of him. They all did the same.

"I'll begin," said Alderan, closing his eyes.

Simon did not close his eyes as most of the others did. He wanted to see what Alderan was going to do. He didn't see anything, but he felt it. First, it was like a pulse that came from his neighbor's hand and into his body, then out his other hand to the next person. Next came an onslaught of ideas, feelings, and images. He was receiving everything Alderan knew about their case: the contents of the journals, all the timelines, and family trees.

He heard Lianon say he was going next. Again there was a pulse and massive influx of information: his initial investigation into the children's parentage, his conversations with the Radcliffs, then his discussions with the Council. Aeriearie, Rumena, and Celenious went next and presented the day's findings. Saruir shared the other Council members' findings related to the artifacts' investigation and current suspects.

Devlin said he would give it a try. Saruir told him to simply open his mind and Alderan would pull the information and send it around. Lola went next.

Edward offered his mind as well, then Phyllis. They ended with Simon. That's where they found out about his discussions with Archibald, his trips through time in search of information, as well as a cure. He felt naked, exposed. But he knew this was not the time to be stingy with information. Besides, if he lived among the High Elves, they would have access to his mind anyway.

Once the operation was completed, they unclasped hands and everyone seemed to be digesting this information. Edward had passed out in his chair, poor man. Clearly, this was too much for a non-magical human to process. Simon could hardly believe the quantity of data that had just been shoved into his brain.

Lianon nodded to himself. "I guess that explains where Lola and Devlin got their magical abilities. When Annie bound the twins' powers, they were safely tucked away until another set of siblings could pick them up again. Lady Evers may have been as powerful as she was because her brother died at birth and then retained all the power for herself. I believe we should expect great things from the next generations of Evers."

Devlin and Lola blushed at this. Devlin coughed and changed the subject back to the matter at hand. "Should we discuss the proposed solution for Mr. Radcliff's successor?"

Simon snapped out of it and said, "I think that's a great idea. Ultimately, it is your decision though, Devlin."

Phyllis agreed, as did Lola. Alderan said he looked forward to the challenge of becoming an attorney.

"How old will you be when you go to Earth?" asked Devlin.

That's a good question, thought Simon. He estimated Alderan to be older than Aeriearie, but younger than Rumena, according to their demeanor. They all looked the same age as him.

"I shall be approximately twenty-eight human years," he replied.

Bingo, thought Simon. "So if you do the internship, you'll be a lawyer around thirty-one. That's a reasonable age."

"Should we wake Mr. Radcliff?" asked Rumena.

"I think you should let him sleep. Though perhaps he could be moved to a more comfortable resting place," suggested Phyllis.

"Indeed," said Saruir. "Alderan, will you take Mr. Radcliff to your dwelling and install him in your guest chambers. When he wakes, offer him nourishment, explain that the Evers have agreed to the new terms, and go back to his office with him so the new contract may be drafted. While you are there, you can familiarize yourself with the contents of the Evers' files. You may both return here when the work is completed."

Alderan nodded and gently picked up the older man. Edward did not rouse as he was carried out of the Council Chamber.

"As for the rest of you, will you join us in our communal meal? You will have time to rest and refresh yourselves," said Saruir.

That's when it occurred to Simon that he had taken no food or drink since arriving this morning. He had no idea how much time had passed. Looking out the window did not provide a clue. He expected to be wiped out after the 'sharing' but truly he felt fine.

"I don't know about my family, but I would be delighted," said Simon.

"Yes, thank you for the invitation," said Phyllis, ever the gracious lady.

Devlin and Lola nodded in agreement.

"I believe you can make your way to your dwelling?" asked Saruir.

"Yes, thank you," said Simon.

"Aeriearie will fetch you when the meal is served," said the Leader and rose from the table.

Everyone rose and dispersed. Simon led his family back to their house. No one said much of anything. When they were in the house, they all dropped into seats in the main area.

Finally, Lola broke the silence. "What do you think we're going to eat?"

They all started laughing.

CHAPTER 28

DEVLIN

AERIEARIE LED them to a large open-air domed structure, which she called the Feasting Pavilion. Celenious had shown him how to block others from his thoughts, and it seemed to be working so far. If it wasn't, Aeriearie was being very discreet.

She was so beautiful. Which was funny, because all the High Elves looked rather similar. How could one stand out so much to him? He didn't really care about that answer, he could just look at her all day and all night.

Devlin looked up and searched the sky for the sun. He found none. It was simply light.

"Aeriearie, if there is no time, nor is there apparently a sun, does it ever get dark?"

"It is dark when they agree it should be dark," answered Lola. "Just like it is time to eat when they agree that it is."

Phyllis and Simon looked up in surprise, searching for the nonexistent sun.

"But what if people get hungry earlier or later? Or grow tired?" said Devlin. He and Celenious had not covered this.

"Ancient and High Elves never get tired nor hungry. We have a communal meal once per day as a social gathering. We eat very little.

We are sustained by the energy of the island, and the sharing of thoughts and feelings," Aeriearie replied.

"Wow," said Lola. "No wonder everyone is slim and strong. You all eat exactly the same thing and fast most of the day. That's actually a trend back home right now. They call it intermittent fasting."

"Fasting has always been around, Lola," replied Phyllis. "For health, political, and religious reasons."

"Yes, Mother and I would fast from Palm Sunday to Good Friday, every Easter," said Devlin.

Aeriearie gave him an approving look. Devlin beamed.

"That's six days!" cried Lola. "I could never go for six days without eating!"

Devlin laughed. "I'm not sure you could go for twenty-four hours without eating. But you'll get your chance to train for it while we are here," he teased.

"But it won't be proper training, since I'm in an Elf body and can obviously skip a meal. I don't know how long in human time we've been here, but this feels like the evening meal to me," said Lola.

"Come, they are waiting," said Aeriearie, putting an end to the conversation.

There was a large oblong table in the center of the Pavilion covered with food. Devlin had assumed they were vegetarian, but there was also fish and some type of fowl. There were fruits and vegetables, though a lot of the produce was unfamiliar to him. There was also bread in various sizes. There were no serving utensils, but everything was bite-size. He saw no plates.

Aeriearie told them to wait a moment. She came back carrying a tray of pewter plates and cups. "These are yours to use for the duration of your stay. You may cleanse them in your dwelling and bring them back to tomorrow's feast and those that follow."

They each took a plate and cup. She took them around the buffet and explained the offerings, providing descriptions of the taste of the unfamiliar foods. Once their plates were full, she showed them where they could fill their cups. There were two large silver vats with taps.

One contained wine, and the other held water. They all filled their cups with water.

"And now it's time to socialize. Feel free to roam around the room and join groups. Everyone will welcome you and most are looking forward to interacting with you. I will look in on you a bit later," she said and left them to join another party.

Devlin looked around the room. There were no tables or chairs, per se. But there were benches along the perimeter of the Pavilion. Most groups were seated in groups on cushions on the floor, either balancing their plates on their knees or placing them beside them on the floor.

"Shall we split up?" suggested Devlin.

Phyllis and Simon nodded, but Lola looked horrified.

"Why don't we girls stick together," suggested Phyllis with a wink.

Simon went to join Lianon—apparently, they had a few things to discuss. Phyllis and Lola went to join Rumena's party.

Devlin was not going to follow Aeriearie like a lovesick puppy. He scanned the room and saw a group of High Elves who were looking intently at each other but did not appear to be talking. He could practice his telepathy skills.

CHAPTER 29
PHYLLIS

LOLA AND PHYLLIS approached Rumena who introduced them to the people she was eating with. They were friendly, and the younger High Elves asked about Lola's life on Earth.

As they all seemed familiar with social human dynamics, Phyllis asked if they lived in family groups, if they went to school, and what they did for work in the community.

She was told that Ancient and High Elves mated in a similar fashion to humans—that is, some paired off, some did not. Some had children, some did not. There were no gender or species limitations to mating, though there was an age limitation. High Elves had to be one hundred and fifty years old before choosing a mate. It was roughly the equivalent of sixteen years of age for humans. That was also the recommended age for drinking wine, choosing an occupation, and moving out of the family dwelling.

Dwellings belonged to the community and were free to live in. When a High Elf's status changed, they moved to another community.

Those who did not choose mates lived in a community of single High Elves, sharing a dwelling with three others. Communities were created from occupations. Scientists lived with other scientists and so on. It made life easier as they had more in common.

Those who chose a mate, but did not wish to have children lived in a community of paired High Elves. In these communities, the dwellings were smaller, only large enough for two people. The pairs were placed randomly in these communities.

Those who chose a mate and had children lived in communities for families. They too were placed randomly. There were playgrounds and schools in these communities. Children stayed with the primary caregiver for the equivalent of the first five years of their lives. They went to Primary School from age five to twelve where they were taught reading, writing, mathematics, science, oral proficiency, philosophy, history, and geography. They also learned to meditate, swim, hike, and a practice similar to yoga.

In Primary School, there were no graded assessments. Students worked until they mastered the skills. They were not grouped by age or skill. Students were free to work independently, in pairs, or in small groups of like-minded students. The teacher's time was spent with students needing clarification or who were struggling. Primary school ended when a student had mastered all the necessary skills to move on to the next phase of life.

At this point, they were assessed for strengths and interests. From this assessment, suitable occupations were suggested. The student took the next two to three years to explore these professions, spending time observing those who did them, and interviewing them. Once they had a clear choice, they were placed with a Master in that field and became their apprentice for as long as was required to master the occupation and work independently.

The community provided everything they needed: shelter, sustenance, attire, tools, knowledge, and opportunities for growth. There was no need for the exchange of money.

Ancient and High Elves were never sick, were happy most of the time, and there was very little conflict. If a disagreement hindered the decision-making process, a third party was requested to act as moderator. If the decision concerned the entire community, it was presented to the Council.

Council members were elected by the community members and

served a term of one hundred years. It included representatives from each of the main occupations: knowledge, science, food production, wellness, land maintenance, and engineering. Two of the Council members were chosen to be emissaries for foreign exchange. They sat on various Councils, one of which was the Council of Earthly Magical Beings, which oversaw the collective Councils of Elders for Travelers.

Phyllis was impressed by this seemingly advanced civilization. She assumed they were similar to the Limurians or the Atlanteans who once lived on Earth. But she couldn't help feeling that there was just too much sameness. Clearly, it could not work on Earth. By definition, humans were messy, complicated, contrary, and unique. Getting them to agree to disagree was a major undertaking. And as petty and often immature as they acted, Phyllis thought she preferred being one of them.

It did, however, make for a fascinating dinner conversation.

CHAPTER 30

LOLA

DESPITE BEING ENTHRALLED by the description of the High Elves' way of living, Lola's food antenna poked up. Turning, she saw they had changed the spread on the buffet table. She needed to investigate.

She looked at Phyllis and waited for a lull in the conversation. Catching her attention, she nodded to the buffet, smiling and pumping her eyebrows. Phyllis smiled at Lola and gave her a quick nod. They thanked their new friends for the company and the conversation and promised to visit with them again soon.

As they walked towards the buffet, they saw both Devlin and Simon making their way there as well, as were some of the High Elves.

"Fancy meeting you here," exclaimed Lola.

"As soon as I saw the food had changed, I knew you would be looking for dessert," replied Devlin.

"I saw Devlin getting up, then checked on the two of you. I decided to follow suit," said Simon.

They made a lap around the table. The food seemed more familiar. There were fruits such as grapes, persimmons, figs, apples, and dates. There were different cheeses, new types of bread, and a selection of olives. Lola searched for cakes, pies, or cookies. Or anything sweet, really. As though seeing her disappointment, Headmaster Lianon walked up to her and offered a larger fruit, cut in half.

"It is called jungle fruit. It grows here on Summerset. The taste is similar to dragon fruit," explained the Headmaster, urging her to take it.

Lola thanked him and looked at the fruit suspiciously. For one thing, she had never tasted dragon fruit and the name was ominous. For another, fruit was never a proper dessert—it was a snack, or part of breakfast. She put her goblet and plate down on the table, and took the fruit, unsure if she should use the spoon or bite it like an orange. One look at Phyllis told her to take her spoon. She dug into the fruit—it was soft and easy to scoop out. Bringing it up to her nose, she sniffed it. It smelled good, sweet. She smiled and looked up to see everyone was observing her intently.

"Lola the explorer," joked Devlin.

Lola stuck out her tongue at him and immediately blushed as she realized the Headmaster was still with them.

The spoon finally made its way to her mouth, which closed around it. She first registered the smooth creaminess, like that of a thick custard. It was sweet, but in a peppery kind of way, though not spicy like a chili—the way it's hard to say if nutmeg is sweet or savory. She didn't have anything to compare it to, but she knew she liked it. And the others knew it too, by the grin that spread across her face.

"That's amazing! Thank you so much, Headmaster," she said, digging into the fruit for another spoonful.

"What does it taste like?" asked Phyllis, curious.

"The closest I can say is vanilla custard; the English kind," replied Lola, scraping the sides of the empty fruit while looking around for another half to wolf down.

The Headmaster smiled in amusement, stretched an arm towards a bowl, and grabbed another half for her.

"Be aware that overindulging in jungle fruit leads to restless sleep and digestive upset. I would not advise eating more than one per day," he said, and then explained that he was retiring for the evening.

Phyllis and Devlin said they were stuffed. They went to the drinks area and found some tea. Simon tried the jungle fruit but found it a bit too sweet for his taste. He took Lola's cup and went to get them some of the tea too. It was clear and green, but it tasted like a blend of licorice and basil.

They went to sit on a bench facing the lake. Ancient and High Elves were starting to leave, and soon the horizon started to dim. It was like the color was draining from the sky. What used to be a bright blue gradually gave way to darkening shades of gray until it was pitch black. It was pretty to look at, but not nearly as breathtaking as a sunset on Earth. The turnover was about midway between the sky and the lake like a blind being pulled down when it occurred to Lola that perhaps they should head home while it was still light enough to see the path.

She rose, about to share her revelation with her family, when they too rose from the bench.

"Let's get home before dark," suggested Simon.

CHAPTER 31

SIMON

WHEN THEY ARRIVED HOME, none of them was very tired. They sat in their living room and chatted about their day, though most of the big things had been shared through the thought exchange. But this was how humans related to one another—through discussion.

One of the things that had not been shared was Simon's decision to stay in Summerset at the end of their two-week stay and take on the job of art professor at The Academy. As he'd hoped, they embraced his decision and were overjoyed that he would not only be healthy but that they could spend time together as a family.

"You realize I may only have another ten years or so," he warned.

"It's more than we ever expected to have, given that you died when we were kids," stated Lola.

"I feel grateful for any time I get to spend with you," replied Devlin, a little choked up.

"Me too, buddy," said Simon, clapping Devlin on the back and giving him a side hug.

"Even though you and I spent our whole lives together, I never tire of having my big brother around. I've missed you terribly these past years. And I'm so very happy you get the chance to spend some time with your children. I know how sad you were before you died," said Phyllis.

The sentence gave Simon the chills. Phyllis remembered him dying, but he hadn't died yet, and he wasn't particularly looking forward to the experience.

"How exactly is that supposed to work?" asked Lola. "I mean, you're supposed to die soonish in your time, right?"

Simon swallowed audibly and said, "I don't know the details, but Headmaster Lianon said they would somehow manipulate the timeline. I'm not sure I want to know exactly what that means. What's clear is that a Simon Evers dies in 2005, while another Simon, me, lives on here."

They remained silent for a while, seeming to contemplate what he'd just said.

When no one spoke, Simon suggested they call it a night. They said their goodnights and went to bed.

CHAPTER 32
DEVLIN

DEVLIN WOKE when he sensed it was light out. It was very disconcerting not knowing what time it was. He had showered before bed and found it very relaxing. He hoped he and Lola would be allowed to visit the Wellness Center. From Phyllis' description, it was certainly worth a visit.

He removed his sleeping attire and folded the garments neatly. He smoothed out the bedcovering and placed his folded stack on top. Calling up the sink, he washed his face and brushed his teeth with the items he had brought from home.

The previous night he had placed the tunic he had worn that day on the back of the chair. It was no longer there. The shoes had disappeared as well. Surely they would be returned after laundering.

Opening the wardrobe, he took the other tunic and put it on. He did the same with the other pair of shoes. Today, the clothing fit his frame perfectly. He raked his fingers through his long hair, wondering if he should brush it. As he found no knots, and he did not have a brush, he put the matter out of his mind. Turning back to the bed, he noticed his pajamas were no longer on the bed.

It occurred to him that the laundry system at the Academy might not be the work of invisible workers in the basement, but simply a magical system borrowed from the High Elves. Either way, it was efficient and he was grateful. He had never liked doing laundry. It always seemed like such a redundant, needless task.

Besides having items laundered, his other favorite aspect of the Academy was the uniform. He loved not having to make a lot of choices with his appearance. It was even better in Summerset as there were no choices at all. One tunic, one pair of shoes. Done.

He looked over his neat room, smiled in contentment, and headed to the main area. Simon was there, staring out at the lake, holding a steaming cup. He turned when Devlin came to stand next to him.

"Did you sleep well, son?" Simon asked.

Devlin beamed at his father and nodded. For his entire life, he had dreamed of sharing such a moment, any moment, with his father. The simple exchange that most people took for granted.

"You?" he asked in reply.

"Better than I have in years," said Simon. "I have a lot to be grateful for this morning," he said, putting his arm around Devlin and giving him a squeeze.

"Is that coffee?" asked Lola, coming into the room.

"No, it's an herbal tea," replied Simon, taking Lola in for a hug.

Devlin gave his sister a hip bump and a smile. He was so happy he could burst.

Lola went to the kitchen console and started tapping. Moments later, Phyllis walked into the room. She headed for the men and gave them each a peck on the cheek, then grabbed Simon's cup and took a sip.

"Yum, what is that called?" she asked, as she went to join Lola in the kitchen. She stroked Lola's hair absently and kissed the top of her head.

"Morning Glory," replied Simon with a chuckle.

"How apt," replied Phyllis and asked Lola to call one up for her. The console asked for Phyllis' cup to be placed on the counter. They had positioned their mess kits on the kitchen table upon arriving the previous night, but these too had disappeared.

Hands on hips, Phyllis exclaimed in confusion, "I was sure I left my things here on the table."

Devlin went to the kitchen area and started opening the cabinets. He found their kits, shiny and clean, and took out the three remaining cups.

"I'll have a Morning Glory too," he said, and placed two cups on the counter, handing the third to Lola.

She tapped the liquids icon, found the Morning Glory tea, and chose two cups. They instantly filled with hot green liquid. Phyllis took their teas and went back to join Simon by the window.

"There's no coffee in here," grumbled Lola.

She came over to look out at the lake too, and they stood there, drinking their tea and enjoying the moment.

Devlin saw Aeriearie walking up the path to their house first. Her hair bounced away in its usual splendor. He couldn't help smiling at her loveliness. He moved away from the others to greet her at the door.

"Good morning," he said as he opened the door.

"Good Morning, Devlin," she replied and laughed as she entered their house. "Good morning, Phyllis, Simon, and Lola," she repeated, and they answered in turn.

"No coffee," Lola said, gesturing to their mugs.

Aeriearie laughed again. "Oh, dear. Do you like the tea, though?"

Lola couldn't help but grin. "Yeah, it's pretty good."

"Are you ready for another day on Summerset?" Aeriearie asked, and they all agreed.

She called up a map on one of the side tables in the main area.

"Eventually, you will know where to go instinctively, but for now here is a map of the central village where we are situated. Phyllis, you will be joining Rumena again at the Knowledge Center"—she pointed to it on the map—"Simon, Lianon is expecting you at his dwelling. Just follow the lake path and turn right at this intersection." She traced the route with her fingers and tapped on the last house of that lane. "Lola and Devlin will come with me to the Science Center for a while, and we'll all meet at the Wellness Center at midday."

When Devlin arrived at the Science Center, Celenious was waiting for him in their little workroom.

"What are we practicing today?" he asked.

"How to use a portal," replied Celenious.

Devlin's eyes grew huge, and he smiled in delight.

"Don't get too excited, we'll start with the island and see how it goes."

Celenious explained that High Elves could open portals to anywhere, from anywhere, simply through intention and by waving their hands in an arc. He demonstrated the procedure for Devlin.

"As you have not yet mastered all of our abilities, you will use the touchpad," explained Celenious.

Devlin, though visibly disappointed, nodded and touched the glass surface on the table. Swiping through the options, he pulled up the Portal app. There were a few locations to choose from. Looking up at Celenious for confirmation, Devlin tapped the lake.

A portal appeared on the wall of the room. The boys got up and Celenious motioned for Devlin to go first. It was a different feeling than using his door. Going through the door to Summerset had felt like walking through any other door. But going through the portal felt like walking through runny glue and he felt like his insides had been rearranged differently en route.

He shook it off and marveled at his surroundings. They were on the other side of the lake. There was a path here as well, and they started walking down it.

Celenious explained how the portals were equivalent to the Sphere in terms of possibilities. Since few Travelers had psychic abilities, the High Elf had designed the Spheres to retain trip information and share it with other Spheres. The accumulated knowledge was available at the Knowledge Center if Devlin wanted to absorb it.

"I am very interested in that knowledge," said Devlin eagerly.

"Alright. I'll take us to the Knowledge Center and from there you can take us to our next destination," suggested Celenious.

They arrived directly in one of the private glassed-in rooms. Celenious asked Devlin to select their next location while he retrieved the cube. When he returned, Devlin asked him why children went to school and apprenticed with older High Elves if all that was required was to absorb a cube or two.

"Children's brains don't have enough connections to fully process all the knowledge of the Collective. Neuronal connections are made through learning. The more they learn by themselves, the more connections they have," he explained.

"Is that why you had Lola and I visit the school and try out some of the occupations?" asked Devlin.

"Yes. Though you are both grown and have extra connections due to your magical abilities, the connections you make while you are here will be stronger and remain after you revert back to your human form," said Celenious.

"I wish I'd been able to absorb the contents of the Summer Program the way Phyllis did!" exclaimed Devlin.

"Perhaps, but those intense two weeks with your sister likely contributed to the awakening of your abilities. You both created an important number of connections in a short amount of time due to the neutrality of the world and the lack of distractions," he said.

"What do you mean by neutrality?" asked Devlin.

"The Academy is a pocket world. It was created by the High Elves. Though it may resemble Earth in many respects, it is not subjected to the same Laws of Physics. For example, though there is some gravity, there is not as much as on Earth. This removes a measure of resistance, making learning easier," he explained.

He placed the cube in front of Devlin. "Ready?"

Devlin nodded and grasped the cube on either side, closing his eyes. Once he'd absorbed the contents, he released it and opened his eyes.

"That was incredible! Will I remember all of this when I get home?" he asked.

"The details will not be as vivid, but yes," replied Celenious.

"I feel old. Like I have personally visited each of those worlds over the last decade," said Devlin wearily.

"That is exactly how you would feel if you had been the one to visit all of those worlds. However, the collection of visits spans more than one hundred years. It's normal for you to feel a little out of sorts. Absorbing experiences is a little more encompassing than absorbing knowledge. For a human, it would be like experiencing each of their past lives all at once, though that would also be confusing on an emotional level," explained Celenious.

Devlin nodded silently. He closed his eyes again and took a deep breath while rolling his shoulders and rotating his head. When he felt more relaxed, he shook it off and said, "I think I understand how to open a portal now. Instead of practicing a few more times, could we go for a walk in the jungle? Is it safe?"

"Yes, it's safe if we stay on the path. That is an excellent suggestion. Will you do the honors?" asked Celenious.

Devlin used the touchpad to call up a portal to the jungle.

As soon as they went through, Devlin felt better. The air, though still sweet, had an added earthiness to it. Devlin took multiple deep breaths and relaxed. Celenious explained that the path would take them all the way to the cliffs overlooking the ocean.

"The hike there and back should take a few hours and will not be very strenuous," said Celenious.

"Sounds perfect," said Devlin, and they set off.

CHAPTER 33
LOLA

ON THEIR SECOND day in Summerset, she spent the morning working on various extrasensory abilities. Once they had mastered the basics, Aeriearie took her to the Knowledge Center. Phyllis was in a see-through room with Rumena but did not see Lola as her eyes were closed. Lola was very excited to try the cube-absorbing thing. Though she understood the gist of it from Phyllis' recounting, Aeriearie still took her through the process. She had her wait in one of the meeting rooms while she fetched some cubes for her. When she came back, she placed one in front of Lola.

"These contain everything you need to master all the extrasensory abilities. Since you have the predisposition, and you have some skill, it should be easy to absorb," she said.

Lola took a deep breath and braced herself for the experience. When she took hold of the box, she felt like she had both hands on a live wire. It was over in an instant, but the best way she could describe it was that scene in the movie *Paul* where Paul shares his memories with Ruth. Except that Lola didn't faint. But now she understood why they were meeting at the Wellness Center. She was ready to call it a day.

The Wellness Center was like the best spa in the Universe. True, Lola had never been to a spa, but she was sure this was the best. After showering and donning robes and slippers, the whole family met in an atrium. Once their party was complete, Aeriearie told them she had other things to attend to and hoped they enjoyed themselves.

They followed one of the attendants down two flights of stairs, then down a long hallway to a thick stone door. Lola turned to Devlin and made big eyes at him. He nudged her forward.

The door opened into a cave. A cave! The attendant grabbed a torch and told them to follow her. She explained the cave contained warm mineral pools they could soak in. There was a choice between one large pool that would accommodate everyone or individual pools.

When none of them answered, she gave the torch to Simon and said, "I'll be back to fetch you later."

"Don't you need the torch to light your way?" he asked.

She was almost at the door when she replied, "No, and neither do you. Your eyes will adjust. But the one called Lola is afraid of the dark and I thought it would alleviate her discomfort."

She opened the door and left before Lola could refute the allegation. It was, of course, true, but much too embarrassing to be dignified with a response.

"I know we all have almost identical bodies, but I'm not sure I'm ready to soak naked with my family just yet," exclaimed Lola.

No one disagreed with her, and Simon went to put the torch back in the holder by the door. When he came back, their eyes had adjusted to the darkness. They walked around the cave and each chose the pool that most called to them and were sufficiently dispersed that no one's privacy felt encroached upon.

Lola's pool was surrounded by stalagmites and very private. She dropped her robe and stepped into the water. It was warm, but not too hot. The pool wasn't very deep, and one of the rock walls had been chiseled into a smooth bench. She sat down and marveled at the feeling of the water. It was so relaxing despite the absence of bubbles.

Now she knew why there weren't any bathtubs in the house. This was so much better.

She closed her eyes and rested her head on the stone wall. She must have fallen asleep because she heard her name being called, saying it was time to go. Already?

There was no one around; she got out of the pool and put on her robe and slippers. She looked around to get her bearings and headed towards the door. Simon and Devlin were already there with the attendant. When Phyllis joined them, they all went back upstairs.

Back in the atrium, the attendant outlined the possible treatments they could receive. Both Lola and Phyllis chose massages, while Devlin opted for a mud bath, and Simon a salt scrub.

Lola was in heaven. The mineral water soak had relaxed her, but this was like the cherry on top. This was only her second massage, but it was clearly out of this world. She couldn't believe how incredible it felt to have your hands and feet massaged. She fell asleep again and woke up alone in the room. She stretched under the blanket and sighed. She could get used to this.

CHAPTER 34

PHYLLIS

PHYLLIS HAD LOST track of time. After the third day, they all blurred together. They would get up, get dressed, have tea together, then head out for the day. The High Elves had assessed Lola and Devlin and given them the option of exploring occupations like the other youngsters.

Devlin spent his days at the Science Lab with Celenious and Aeriearie. Phyllis knew he was genuinely interested in science, otherwise, she may have objected. Lola shadowed the Processing Team at the Knowledge Center.

As for Phyllis, she had completed her absorption of all five installments of the Summer Program and was now up to speed with the children. Simon had begun the process as well, in preparation for his new job. He had left with Lianon for a tour of the Academy.

Now, Phyllis had moved on to learning languages—specifically Elvin. She had also requested the ability to communicate through telepathy as it was clear all the Evers had the predisposition. She enjoyed practicing both with Rumena and her other new friends.

Every night, they made a point to sit with new people. It was easier for her now that she could speak their language, though many of them were hoping to practice English. As a compromise, Phyllis spoke

French, Italian, and Spanish to those who had absorbed the languages and it was great fun.

She did not go to the Wellness Center every day, as that would have taken away from its specialness. Instead, she sometimes took a book outside and sat near the lake to read. Now that she had mastered Elvin, she was able to appreciate their endless collection of sonnets.

One day, as she was daydreaming by the lake, Simon came to find her to let her know Edward and Alderan had returned with the paperwork. They made their way to the Council Pavilion and found the children had also heard the news. They went in together and greeted the attorney warmly. He blinked at them, still getting used to their Elvish appearance.

They reviewed the new contract and the paperwork together. Everything seemed to be in order. Devlin, as Custodian and official Head of the Family, put his signature on all the documents.

Alderan had been introduced to Edward Sr. who had wholeheartedly embraced the idea. He was then introduced to the staff as Edwards' new paralegal, working exclusively on the Evers' files due to his participation in the Reading Law Program. There were no objections, and so far, Alderan was doing well.

They had found him an apartment, furnished it, and went shopping for appropriate attire. Edward said he was having a lot of fun, even if Alderan was finding a lot of their tasks to be tedious in the extreme. Though he had absorbed information blocks about life on Earth, specifically in the Southern USA, he was still flabbergasted that he had to shop for food, prepare meals, and clean up after himself, three times per day. Having to select different clothing every day so as not to arouse suspicion from the fashion police, then having to wash, dry, and fold his clothing also seemed unnecessary.

"And all of this is to be repeated every single day!" he wailed. "It is such a waste of time and energy."

After a few days of this, Edward had put the poor guy out of his misery and got him a cook/housekeeper. He explained that he was not required to eat breakfast or lunch every day if he didn't want to, as a lot of people just didn't have time and skipped it altogether. To this Alderan had replied, "But I'm always hungry and I'm always tired."

The Evers family laughed good-naturedly and told him he would get used to it.

"At least I no longer get lost on public transit," he exclaimed proudly.

That got another round of laughter. They were chatting about Alderan's experience on Earth, and their experience there as High Elves when Saruir entered, followed by the other Council members.

"We have news about the investigation," said Saruir as everybody was seated.

Just then, two High Elves came into the room and were seated at the table. They were obviously twins. As much as the High Elves resembled each other, these two were identical. Not only were they beautiful, but their appearance was even more striking due to the gowns they wore, a stark contrast to the sober tunics the humans were all wearing.

"I believe Lola and Devlin have met our latest arrivals, but for those of you who do not know them, they are Lady Samsara, Traveling Professor at the Academy, and Lady Mathilda, Dean of Admissions at the McTavish International Academy of Magical Sciences," he said as he gave the floor to Lady Mathilda.

"Hello, everyone, and thank you for having me. It's been ages since I've attended a Council meeting. Now I will try to be as succinct as possible. My sister, Lady Samsara, and Headmaster Lianon approached me about someone who had previously attended McTavish, an Ivan Lazarus," she began, pausing for effect.

Phyllis saw that this woman spent most of her time with humans and had clearly adopted a more flamboyant personality than her fellow High Elves. She smiled in spite of herself. She was a spitfire.

"I remembered Ivan well. He was always getting into trouble and was repeatedly being suspended for unsanctioned use of magic outside the school walls. I was able to provide a list of known 'associates' to the investigation team. As it were, the band of miscreants had established their lair in London. Lady Samsara and I were able to seize five

Spheres, ten Time Watches, and an impressive collection of Keys, Wands, and other magical artifacts. We brought them back here with us," she exclaimed.

There were whispers around the table. Phyllis wondered what the other magical artifacts were.

"Thank you, ladies, for your part in the retrieval of priceless and dangerous artifacts; they will be safe here," replied Saruir.

Next, he gave the floor to Thanin, one of the High Elves on the investigation team.

"We were able to apprehend the culprits and they will be put before the Council of Magical Earthly Beings for sanctioning. Suffice it to say that both the Magical and the Traveler communities can rest assured that justice will be done and that they are safe from harm."

"What will happen to the Callahans?" asked Lola.

"Aidan has been placed under House Arrest pending his hearing with the Council. His Key has been revoked permanently. For her part in the operation, Arabella's Key has been revoked temporarily by the Custodian," answered Thanin.

"But that's Tom!" exclaimed Lola.

"He has been found innocent in this situation, having only been told about it after the fact and having immediately contacted Headmaster Lianon to receive assistance. The sister, Tabitha, appears to have been completely unaware that anything was going on," he explained.

Lola sagged with relief in her chair. Phyllis was glad. She knew Lola was quite taken with the boy. She wasn't overly fond of the mother or the sister, but Tom was a lovely young man.

"Does that mean we can go home now?" asked Lola.

"Are you not enjoying your stay in Summerset?" asked Saruir, tongue in cheek.

"Yes, sir, of course, I am," Lola stammered, feeling like she was blushing but sure no color appeared on her High Elf skin. "It's just that school starts in a few days and I was looking forward to spending some time at home before setting off again."

"As well you should; there's no place like home!" exclaimed Lady Mathilda.

To which all the humans burst out laughing. Alderan had to explain the reference to the other High Elves.

"Indeed," replied Saruir, amused. "Yes, Lola, you and your family can go home."

"I'll be staying on, of course. Since Headmaster Lianon is going back to work, I'll be heading to the Academy on a daily basis, but I'll see you all on Orientation day," said Simon.

"Splendid," exclaimed Saruir. "Will our guests join us for the evening Feast?"

He looked at the sisters and at Edward. They all agreed to meet at the Pavilion in a little while.

"The children and I will depart in the morning if that is alright with everyone," announced Phyllis. Lola and Devlin nodded. It was to be their last night in Summerset.

CHAPTER 35

SIMON

LADY SAMSARA and Lady Mathilda were very popular at the Feast that evening. Simon was looking for a discreet way of asking where they had acquired their titles when Lola solved the dilemma by asking them outright.

"Both of us were always fascinated with Earth from a very young age," began Lady Samsara. "When it was time to choose occupations, we both opted to become teachers. Mathilda taught Geography and I taught History."

"While the sisters were competent and beloved, it became apparent that they were not reaching their full potential," interrupted Saruir. "My predecessor, Baltaran, while attending a meeting of the Council for Earthly Beings, met a couple who could not have children. She was a witch, and he was a Traveler. It was the first time such a union had come to light, and we initially thought that was the reason they could not have children. Since hearing the Evers' tale, the hypothesis has been put to rest. Anyhow, though by Earthly standards the girls were no longer children, they were the perfect age to be sponsored and launched into London society in 1905."

"You see, our new family were not only magical beings, they were also part of the nobility, which is why they held a seat on the Council.

Lord and Lady Davenport had such a social standing that they were invited to all the biggest events of the season," explained Mathilda, holding everyone's attention.

"When we arrived, however, we realized our schooling in Summerset had not prepared us for the rigors of a London season," added Samsara. "We arrived in August 1905 and spent the following four and a half months being instructed in the arts: music, singing, dance, painting, and needlepoint."

"It was a good thing we had absorbed the necessary language, history, geography, philosophy, and culture knowledge before we arrived, otherwise it might have taken years to get us ready," exclaimed Mathilda.

"We were launched as Lady Mathilda Davenport and Lady Samsara Davenport after being legally adopted by our new parents," concluded Samsara.

"Were either of you married during your time on Earth?" asked Phyllis.

"No. But we attended all the balls and major events, wore incredible gowns, and met legions of eager suitors," answered Mathilda dreamily.

"We decided, instead, to enroll at Bedford College, part of the University of London, where we both obtained our Bachelor of Arts in 1909. Mathilda accepted a teaching position at McTavish and I headed for the Academy. The rest, as they say, is history," concluded Samsara.

"What a fascinating tale," exclaimed Edward, clearly starstruck by the two ladies.

The group broke up then, and Simon stayed with Edward and Alderan. Simon told Edward about his decision to stay in Summerset and his new position at The Academy.

"Have you thought of what they will call you?" asked Edward.

"I assume Professor is the standard title," replied Simon.

"Well, you can't be Simon Evers and look like a High Elf, now can you!" exclaimed Edward.

"Oh, I guess you're right. The students are humans, and I'm supposed to be dead," mused Simon.

"And both your children are attending school. I doubt any of you are eager to broadcast that bit of information," replied Edward.

"Goodness, you're right again. I clearly hadn't thought it through," said Simon. "Any suggestions?"

"How about a combination of your ancestors' names?" suggested Edward.

"You wouldn't happen to have our family tree with you?" replied Simon with a laugh.

Alderan, who was taking his shadowing duties seriously by following Edward everywhere he went, apologized for interrupting then provided a few options. "Here are possible male names from your ancestry: Ambrose, Archibald, Augustus, Bartholomew, Blaine, Davis, Elliot, Greer, Hardy, Harrison, John, Landon, Magnus, Marcus, Orville, Percy, Preston, Victor, and Warwick."

"That's a lot to choose from!" replied Simon. "Perhaps I should enlist my family's help."

Simon turned and looked for Phyllis and the children. He decided to practice his new telepathy skills and called them over. It worked! In turn, they each looked up from their conversations, excused themselves, and made their way to him.

"I need a new name. I can't be Simon Evers at the Academy. Alderan, would you be so kind as to repeat my options?" asked Simon and Alderan immediately complied.

They all took a minute to think about it.

"How about Magnus Preston?" suggested Phyllis.

"I like it," said Simon.

"What about Ambrose Harrison," tried Devlin.

"Also a good option," replied Simon.

Lola was still thinking, tapping a finger under her nose.

"Those are great. But you'll be wearing a High Elf suit, right?" she asked.

Simon nodded.

"Most of the teachers go by 'Professor' followed by their last name, except for Headmaster Lianon and Lady Samsara, who go by title plus first name. How about an anagram of your real name that sounds

Elvish? Like Minos, Monis, Somin, Sinom, Nisom, Nimos," suggested Lola.

"Professor Somin sounds a bit Elvish," replied Phyllis.

"I agree," replied Simon. "What does everybody think of Somin?"

They all agreed it would suit him, and gave a toast to the new Professor Somin, Visual Arts teacher at the Academy.

Saruir approached them and asked if he could propose a toast to the family, seeing as it was their last night in Summerset. They agreed. He went to stand in front of the buffet table and motioned for them to follow. He raised his hands and everyone turned their attention to him.

"Dearest community, tonight we must say our farewells to these wonderful humans. Edward Radcliff has agreed to foster Alderan on Earth and teach him his trade so that Alderan can take over his duties after his apprenticeship," he began and there was a cheer from the assembly. "Simon Evers is joining our community and will take over as Arts Professor at the Academy and will henceforth be known as Somin." More cheers from the High Elves.

"And last but not least, let us thank Phyllis, Lola, and Devlin, for blessing us with their unique perspectives," said Saruir. Then he raised his glass and said, "You will always be welcome in Summerset."

Everyone raised their glass to toast the humans. Saruir asked if anyone wanted to say anything and, since no one else was volunteering, Phyllis decided to address their new friends.

"On behalf of my family, and Edward who is an honorary member, I thank you for your hospitality. It has been a great honor to spend some time in your beautiful land, getting to know not only your culture but the amazing inhabitants we hope we can now call friends. Do let us know if any of you wish to visit us on Earth, we would be glad to have you," she said.

There was more cheering and clapping. When it died down, Phyllis, Lola, and Devlin went to say more personal goodbyes to Aeriearie, Celenious, and Rumena. When the sky turned to gray, they headed back to the house.

In the morning, the reality of their departure sunk in. Simon was going to miss them. Phyllis and the children wore their Earth clothes and had resumed their human forms. He hugged each of them tightly, but he hugged Phyllis a little longer.

"I'll see you in a few days, Simon. I'll be accompanying the children to Orientation," said Phyllis.

"I know, but I'll be Professor Somin then, not your brother. So even if you come to visit every Sunday, it won't be the same," replied Simon with emotion.

"We'll see you over the Holidays," said Phyllis, pulling him down so she could kiss his cheek.

"And we will see you at school," said Devlin.

"Surely you'll have an office we can visit if we want to speak privately?" queried Lola.

"Of course, I've already seen it. It's amazing!" said Simon.

The children laughed and explained it was probably like all the other teachers' offices: adjacent to their classroom, equipped with a desk, some bookshelves, and two armchairs in front of the fireplace.

"It also has a private bathroom," said Simon. "And it has a southern exposure with a lot of light. I've already set up my easel by the window."

"Perhaps I could send some of your things from the mansion; perhaps a few paintings you've completed since you died. It would be a shame to leave them stacked in your alcove," suggested Phyllis.

"Lovely idea, thank you, Phyllis," said Simon, giving his sister another squeeze.

"Where will you live after we've gone?" asked Lola.

"The Headmaster offered me a room. As a Council member, he has a house to himself. Since he usually stays in his rooms at the Academy during the school year, I'll have the house to myself. And since I'll be home in Virginia during the school holidays, he'll be by himself. It's an efficient solution," said Simon.

He had packed his belongings to take with him to the new house after his family had left.

Since they couldn't take a portal directly from the house, they walked to the Council Pavilion and entered. Simon opened his bag and gave his Key to Devlin.

"That was the condition," said Simon. "The Repository, Archives, and artifacts went home with Edward and Alderan this morning. If you need them, you know where to find them."

Devlin and Lola nodded.

Simon opened a portal for them and waved them off. "See you soon!"

CHAPTER 36

DEVLIN

THEY ARRIVED home in the upstairs hallway. Devlin checked his watch; it was Tuesday, September first, at eight a.m. They had been gone for nine days and still had five days before they needed to report to school. *Perfect*, thought Devlin.

"I'm starving!" exclaimed Lola.

Phyllis and Devlin laughed but said they were hungry too. They agreed to drop their things and head to the kitchen to make some breakfast. That's where Sally found them when she arrived at nine a.m. Since the family was away, she didn't have to come in early to prepare breakfast.

"Why didn't you ask me to come in, Ms. Evers? I could have had breakfast ready for y'all," she clucked, shooing them out of the kitchen.

"I'm sorry, Sally, we arrived in the middle of the night, too late to let you know, and we only just woke up," replied Phyllis.

"Well, I'm here now. You go on to the dining room, and I'll bring everything out to you," replied the housekeeper.

Lola refilled her coffee cup and grabbed one of the blueberry muffins they had defrosted. Devlin grabbed one too, and they headed for the dining room. Soon after, Sally started setting things up on the sideboard. They patiently waited for her to complete the setup, thanked her, and loaded up their plates.

It was like they hadn't eaten in a week. Devlin didn't ever remember being this hungry, even when he was a growing teenager. Even Phyllis, who usually had fruit with a little yogurt, carried a plate full of bacon and eggs back to her seat. Lola's plate looked normal: full to the brim. Devlin chuckled and sat down at the table. They ate in silence for quite some time, only getting up for juice, tea, or coffee refills.

"This would have been the ideal opportunity to reduce your caffeine consumption," suggested Devlin. "Since you haven't had any in nine days."

"I was in an Elf body; they don't need caffeine. I, a mere human, require coffee to function at a socially acceptable level," snapped Lola.

"I see your point," replied Devlin, exchanging an amused look with Phyllis.

Phyllis, having completed her herculean feast, announced she was going to look at messages and emails, then head to her room to rest.

"I was fine when we arrived, but the heavy meal has made me feel sleepy," she said, getting up.

Devlin rose and said, "It is likely the density of Earth and the pull of gravity. I'm sure we'll adjust back soon enough."

Lola rose as well and said she would spend the day floating in the pool to counter the feeling of heaviness. She kissed Phyllis on the cheek, waved at Devlin, and left the room.

"Very clever, darling," replied Phyllis on her way out.

It appeared no one was interested in what Devlin had planned for the day. He went to the kitchen to ask Sally for the daily paper. He took it back to the dining room, grabbed a cup of herbal tea, and took his seat. He would catch up on Virginian affairs, check in with John, and take care of the weekly tasks once Phyllis had vacated the Study.

CHAPTER 37
LOLA

LOLA WENT to her room to get her phone. She put on her bathing suit and a cover-up. She'd check her emails later. She still needed to reply to Jane, and she was sure Jackson would have sent a recap of his trip so far.

Passing through the kitchen, she let Sally know where she would be and asked if they had anything she could use to make a sandwich later on. Sally assured her that Phyllis had gone over the week's menu with her and that she was heading out for groceries.

"I'll make sandwiches for everyone and put them on a plate in the fridge," said Sally.

Lola thanked her and headed to the pool. Her feet felt so heavy. They had learned about grounding in M&M class, but this was an entirely new level of grounding. She hadn't realized how light and graceful she was as a High Elf. Now she just felt awkward.

She grabbed a towel and a bottle of water inside the pool house, dropped her stuff on a chair, and made a beeline for the pool. The water was warm and it felt wonderful to be immersed in it. She let herself float on her back and closed her eyes, pretending she was in the mineral bath back in Summerset. Her eyelids started to feel droopy and she forced herself to stay awake long enough to get out of the pool. It took all the strength she had to climb the stairs out of the pool. She felt even heavier than before. She wrapped the towel around herself, moved her stuff to the side table, put the lounge chair flat, and settled in for a nap.

Someone tugged at her hand. "Lola, wake up. You are going to burn," the voice said.

Confused, Lola lifted her head up. She was lying on her stomach and her neck hurt from having slept in the crook of her arms.

"Jackson?" she croaked.

"No, silly, it is Devlin," replied the voice.

Lola woke up fully then and turned onto her back. For a minute there, she had thought it was Jackson, coming to scold her for not putting on some sunscreen. Of course, she had forgotten. But it was Devlin's turn to scold her, not Jackson.

"I was under the parasol," she mumbled.

"Perhaps you were, an hour ago," he replied, handing her the sunscreen. She took it reluctantly and started to slather some on her arms, legs, and face.

"What time is it?" she asked.

"Lunchtime!" he said, taking a plate from behind his back.

Lola perked up immediately, wiped her hands on the towel, and took the plate from him. There was a tuna sandwich, a pickle, and some salt and vinegar chips—her favorite!

"Thanks, Devlin. Have you eaten already?" she asked.

"Yes, I ate with Phyllis. She has gone to spend the afternoon with Boris. She will be back in time for dinner," he replied, sitting down on the chair beside hers.

"Cool. What have you been up to?" she asked, her mouth full of tuna sandwich.

Devlin gave her a rundown of his morning and she nodded.

"Have you heard from Jackson?" he asked.

"I don't know. I haven't checked my emails, and I fell asleep before

I could check my phone," said Lola, opening her bottle of water. "You?"

"Yes. He sent me a text with a picture of him in Stockholm," replied Devlin, showing Lola the picture.

"Wow! Did he say how the trip was going?" she asked.

"Only that he is having fun," said Devlin.

"Great. Anything for dessert?" asked Lola, putting her empty plate on the table.

Devlin laughed, took a bundle from his pocket, and gave it to Lola.

Lola opened the folded napkin to reveal two oatmeal and raisin cookies. She squealed in delight, which prompted another laugh from Devlin.

"I bet you are already looking forward to dinner," he said with a chuckle.

"I'm stuffed for now, thanks. But if you mean, *Am I looking forward to a home-cooked human meal*, you have no idea," said Lola, picking at the crumbs left in the napkin.

"I may not be a foodie like you, but I admit the food in Summerset was nothing to write home about. However, I did enjoy the Morning Glory tea. I will ask Father to bring some when he comes home for the Holidays," said Devlin.

"Great idea! Maybe he can bring some of that Jungle Fruit too. It was yummy," replied Lola.

Devlin nodded and got up.

"Are you going to put your swimsuit on? The water's nice," said Lola.

"Perhaps later. I am not used to this heat. It is cooler inside. I think I might catch a nap as well," he said with a yawn.

"Okay, see you later," said Lola as he left through the pool house.

Lola grabbed her phone and started scrolling through the texts and messages. Before leaving for Summerset, she had sent a message on their group app to let everyone know she would be away on a family vacation for two weeks. She'd also shot a quick text to Tom.

There were two messages back from Jackson. She opened those first, expecting pictures like Devlin had shown her. She wasn't disappointed. The first one was in Venice. Jackson was on a gondola and had taken a selfie with the gondola driver. The text said simply *Wish you were here.*

The second one was in Paris, at the top of the Eiffel Tower. There were two pics, a selfie of Jackson with the door attendant, and another of the view. This text said *Can't beat this view.*

She moved on to Tom's texts. There were a dozen or so. Some were from before he and Lola had talked on the phone in London. She deleted those. The next few were apologies for what his family had put her through and to reassure her that he had not had anything to do with it, although he did admit that his mother and uncle had encouraged him to get close to her. He explained that he had thought it was because she was new, and an heiress. He explained that her family was not the only one with crazy ideas about suitable matches. He went on to say that he would have sought her out even if they had specifically forbidden him to do it because he had been completely entranced with her from the first moment he saw her. The most recent text was a plea for forgiveness and a promise that his feelings were sincere. They certainly seemed sincere.

But Lola would need input from at least two trusted sources: Phyllis and Sara. As Phyllis was currently out, that left Sara. Sara had sent two texts since she had left for Summerset. The first one read: *OMG! Have you seen the news about Tom?*

The second one read: *Call me ASAP!* It had been sent yesterday. She replied *Yes* to the first one, and *Is now a good time?* to the second one. It was two p.m. here, making it about eight p.m. there.

Sara texted back: *Can I come over*

Lola replied: *Of course, bring a bathing suit.*

A few minutes later, Sara's door appeared on the pool deck. She came through quickly and the door disappeared. Lola got up and rushed over to her friend. Sara was treated to a tight hug. She looked at Lola in surprise.

"Is everything alright?" she asked. "It's the first time you've initiated a hug!"

"I've really missed you!" exclaimed Lola, pulling her friend towards the lounge chairs.

"I've missed you too," said Sara as she removed her cover-up and reclined in the chair, soaking up the Virginia sun. "I could get used to this."

"You won't believe what's been going on!" said Lola.

Lola told Sara everything that had happened since she last saw her at Tom's party. She had a fleeting thought that some of it might best be kept in the family, but this was too big a secret to keep. Dad was on Summerset, Phyllis would likely want to get back to her normal life, and Devlin was great, but he wasn't a girlfriend.

Sara had set a timer on her watch and every twenty minutes they turned over. After the first hour, they took their conversation into the pool.

"Lucky duck, Lola! Do you know how many humans get to visit Summerset? Precious few, that's how many!" she exclaimed. She asked a few clarifying questions and, knowing Lola the way she did, she asked about the food.

"Simple and nutritious," was Lola's reply.

"In other words, horrible!" said Sara and giggled.

"How are things with you? Anything new?" asked Lola.

"Nothing at all to report. Your life is always so much more entertaining than mine," she said.

"Good, because I need your advice about what to do about Tom," said Lola. She reached for her phone and pulled up Tom's texts. She handed her phone to Sara so she could read them.

"He seems sincere," said Sara, handing her back the phone. "Honestly, Lola, even my parents have suggested I befriend people based on their social standing or income. Parents can be such plonkers."

"What the heck is a plonker?" asked Lola through laughter.

"Someone who sucks!" said Sara and Lola laughed even harder.

"You're right. They have such antiquated ideas!" exclaimed Lola.

"I know! My parents still expect me to marry a man! I mean, I like men, but what if I'd been gay? Or didn't want to marry at all?" Sara cried.

"Wow! When I first got here, Phyllis asked me if I had a boyfriend or a girlfriend, so I guess she's a little more open than your parents," replied Lola.

"Anyhow, I think you should give Tom a chance. But unless you miss him terribly, let him sweat it out a few more days. I mean, you said you'd be gone for two weeks and you came home earlier," suggested Sara.

Lola hesitated. "It wasn't his fault, though."

"Do you know what you want to say to him?"

Lola shook her head.

"Then give yourself that time to think about it. Speaking of boys. Now that we've got you sorted, any chance of seeing that pretty brother of yours?" asked Sara, batting her eyelashes sweetly.

"Of course! I'm so sorry I've monopolized you. How long can you stay?" asked Lola.

"You know I don't have a curfew. I'll stay until you send me home," replied Sara, getting out of the pool and grabbing a towel.

"Come on, I have an idea. Do you have your phone?" asked Lola.

"Sure. Why?" asked Sara.

"Let's take a selfie by the pool and you can ask him if he wants to come for a swim," suggested Lola.

"Brilliant!" said Sara. She got her phone, pulled up the camera app, and they shot about ten selfies before they were satisfied. She texted the picture to Devlin with the caption: *Fancy a swim?*

Devlin replied within seconds: *On my way!*

Devlin was clearly not worried about appearing too eager, because his door appeared on the deck and he came out in his bathing suit and flip-flops.

"Hello, ladies. I hear the water is fine," he said as he sent his door back.

"You are so lazy! You could have walked!" laughed Lola.

"Why walk when you can Travel? Besides, I have been to the gym today. I do not require further exercise," he said.

Sara giggled. He approached her, took her hand, and placed a soft kiss upon it.

"You look like a mermaid," he said, and Sara giggled some more.

"Will you join me in the pool?" he asked her.

"Yes, of course," replied Sara. Devlin had not released her hand, and he led her to the pool.

"Are you coming, Lola?" she asked.

"In a minute, I just want to reply to a few texts," lied Lola.

She wanted to give them a little privacy, but not too much, otherwise Devlin would panic at being unchaperoned. She opened the group app and read the messages that had come through since the party. It had been a huge hit.

There was a string about picking majors; James was suddenly second-guessing himself. Everyone told him to pick whatever and change it later. There was a string about Lenora and Keith, Tom's friend. They were still dating, and he had spent a weekend at Lenora's. *Could she finally be serious about a boy?* wondered Lola.

Lola eventually joined Devlin and Sara in the pool and they splashed around and gossiped about their friends. It was a great afternoon and, around five, Sara said it was time for her to go. She was tired and had to get up early the next day to babysit her sisters.

She hugged Lola and Devlin and they promised to stay in touch before school started.

CHAPTER 38

PHYLLIS

PHYLLIS WAS NOT WITH BORIS. She was, in fact, sitting in her physician's reception area waiting for John to pick her up. She had called her doctor that morning requesting an urgent appointment. He had assured her he would squeeze her in, even though she refused to tell him what was wrong over the phone.

As she had been leaving the Council room on their last night in Summerset, Rumena had asked for a private word. Phyllis had expected her friend to express sorrow at her departure and Phyllis was going to propose they stay in touch through letters. Although Rumena had said that was a marvelous idea, she actually had pressing news to impart.

Phyllis looked around, took a deep breath, closed her eyes, and cast her mind back to the conversation.

"What is it?" she had asked. "I know you can't be sick."

"It is not me, it is you!" Rumena replied.

"Good Lord, tell me I don't have cancer!" Phyllis said in a panic, clutching her chest.

Rumena looked horrified and took Phyllis' hand. "Dear friend, no! You are in perfect health."

"What is it, then?" Phyllis asked, looking at her friend intently.

Rumena slowly smiled and Phyllis relaxed her grip on the High Elf's hand.

"You are expecting," Rumena announced. "Isn't it marvelous?"

"Expecting what?" Phyllis asked, confused. And then it dawned on her. Expecting a baby? That couldn't be possible. Well, yes, technically it could be possible.

"But I'm too old!" she exclaimed.

"How old are you, again?" Rumena inquired.

"I'm forty-six," she replied.

Rumena had looked like she was doing the math, or perhaps searching the collective for information about motherhood on Earth.

"You are not too old! Mothers are having babies well past sixty on Earth. I don't even think you qualify for an at-risk pregnancy!" Rumena exclaimed, waving her off.

Phyllis opened her mouth, but no sound had come out. Still clutching her friend's hand, she thought: *I need to sit down but I don't want to attract attention.*

Rumena nodded and led her out of the room and into the hall to sit, away from prying eyes.

"Aren't you happy?" Rumena asked, concern etched on her porcelain face.

"I. I. Yes! Of course, I'm happy. It's just a shock. I've always wanted children, but it never seemed like it was in the cards for me," she said, finding her voice.

"And the father?" Rumena asked.

"Boris! Oh, dear. I have no idea how Boris is going to react. He is older than I am. He's been married before and has grown children who are old enough to have children of their own!" Phyllis explained.

"I see," Rumena replied, waiting for her to continue.

"I don't want to let the others know just yet. I want to sit with this news for a little while if you don't mind," she finally said.

"Of course, I would never disclose information about you to another party unless you authorized me to do so," Rumena quickly assured her.

Phyllis had hugged her and they had gone back into the room to join the others.

When Phyllis had seen her physician, he had given her a physical exam and agreed with Rumena's diagnosis. She was still in the early stages of pregnancy, perhaps a month or so, and was not showing. To be sure, he had her urinate in a cup and asked her to wait for the official results.

The pregnancy was confirmed and he requested she come back in another four weeks. The doctor had outlined her options but did not seem concerned with her age. If Phyllis wanted to continue with the pregnancy, she could expect a normal, healthy pregnancy.

Phyllis thanked Dr. Seymour and said she needed to discuss it with the baby's father. She made an appointment with his secretary and texted John to come to pick her up. Now she was sitting and waiting for him.

No wonder I ate so much at breakfast, she thought.

With the thought of food on her mind, she left the reception area and went next door to the pastry shop while she waited. She had only intended on getting some treats for the children, but she stood transfixed at a two-layer pink and blue cake. The black piping read *We're having Twins!* Phyllis started feeling faint. She asked for an eclair and a glass of water and sat down near the window to keep an eye out for John.

As she waited for her pastry, she tried not to imagine having twins. But obviously, that was impossible. As soon as you tried not to think about a thing, your brain focused solely on it. There had only been one set of twins in their family but perhaps twins ran in Boris' family. She had warmed up to the idea of having a baby. She had never dared to hope. But twins somehow felt a little too overwhelming.

Even if Boris didn't have a heart attack upon hearing the news, and assuming he was happy about it, where were they going to live? In Russia or Virginia? She was about to hyperventilate when the waiter arrived with her eclair and water. She thanked him and downed half the glass.

Then, taking a deep breath, she focused on the eclair. It was perfect.

The chocolate glaze was a neat strip atop the flaky custard-filled pastry. The fork sliced right through it like butter; it was fresh. The first bite hit her tastebuds and she was transported to France, walking down the Champs Élizés.

She tried to savor it, make it last, but after two measured bites, she uncharacteristically took the rest of the eclair and popped the whole thing in her mouth. There was a custard explosion in her mouth and she sighed in pleasure. Then she put her hands to her face in horror. Had anyone seen her stuff the eclair into her mouth?

She turned around to look at the bakery, but there were no other patrons. The clerk was busy in the back. Turning back, she looked outside. There was no one staring at her in disapproval, but she did notice their car pull up in front of the doctor's office.

She rose, left money on the table, and called out her thanks to the clerk on her way out the door.

It was four p.m. when she got back to the house. She went to the kitchen to check on dinner. Sally was just taking a pan of dinner rolls out of the oven. They smelled amazing.

She was beginning to understand how Lola felt. She had just had an eclair in the middle of the afternoon and she hadn't even been hungry. There was no way she was falling prey to the rolls. She had kept her figure this long without rigorous exercise, and she certainly wasn't going to start eating for two. She made a note to ask about prenatal vitamins at her next appointment.

She fled the kitchen and went to her room to soak in the tub and dress for dinner.

CHAPTER 39

SIMON

ON HIS FIRST day of school, the Headmaster presented him with a gift. It was a tunic, but one more elaborate than the one he wore in Summerset. It resembled the one Lianon wore, while still being unique. Simon, or rather Professor Somin, loved it.

There was a mirror in his private bathroom. Though Simon had been living as a High Elf now for over a week, he was still startled upon seeing his reflection. He liked what he saw; it was still him under the pale face and long hair.

He was meeting the staff today. They were having a breakfast meet-and-greet. The Headmaster informed him he was not the only first-time professor. They had recently hired a new Dance Master and a new Philosophy professor.

Lianon had not told him the human-to-other species ratio, while Lola had mentioned only two humans were part of the Summer faculty. Surely there were more on the permanent staff?

Simon then remembered he was no longer part of Team Human. He was now Team High Elf.

Other than Lianon and Samsara, he didn't know if there were other High Elves—he had never asked. As far as anyone would know, he was just another regular High Elf.

He was nervous. Taking one last look at himself in the mirror, he deemed himself presentable and exited the bathroom. He took a leather notebook and a pen and made his way to the Dining Room.

He was thankfully not the first to arrive. Someone had set up a long table, so he placed his notebook and pen on a place setting and made his way to the buffet table, ready to mingle.

The food looked delicious. No wonder Lola raved about it. He debated getting a cup of coffee, first. It too smelled divine. However, when he tasted it, he found the taste to be off somehow, though Lola had assured him it was the best coffee she had ever tasted.

He must have made a face, because Lady Samsara approached and said, "It's not the coffee. It's your taste buds."

"You mean I won't be able to enjoy any of the human food?" asked Simon, unable to hide the disappointment in his voice.

"If you stick to the less processed items, you should be okay," she replied. "Anything that tastes *off* is something unsuitable to our constitution."

"That's clever!" replied Simon. "It would be useful if humans had that."

"Oh, they do. They just don't listen to it!" she replied with a laugh.

"You may have a point," conceded Simon.

"Let me show you where you can get Morning Glory tea," she said and motioned for him to follow her.

Simon perked up immediately. He loved that tea! He'd had a cup this morning before crossing the Portal to his office. Unlike the students who had to Travel to and from the Main Hall, he could use the Portal from his house directly to his office. Talk about a short commute!

He kept his new tunic at work and changed when he arrived. It was always clean and ready for him when he arrived in the morning.

Tea in hand, he followed Samsara around as she introduced him to some of their colleagues. He really was quite grateful to her for doing this. Simon wasn't shy by any means. He was used to attending large events and introducing himself. However, he'd been living a rather solitary life since he fell sick and felt out of practice. Also, he was afraid he might slip up and introduce himself as Simon Evers, out of habit.

This way, he was already Professor Somin to at least a dozen or so faculty members.

The lights blinked. Samsara told him they should head to their seats. He went to the buffet table and placed a few items on his plate before heading to the spot he had reserved for himself. When the Headmaster arrived at the head of the table, everyone rose. Lianon thanked them and told them to be seated.

He gave them a few items of information and then introduced each faculty member. It took some time, as there were easily over fifty teachers seated at the table.

There was a good mix of species and a vast array of expertise. He was happy he had absorbed all the information from the Summer Program because some of the teachers were beyond his imagination and he would not want to offend anyone by saying the wrong thing. He would continue learning new things every weekend at the Knowledge Center.

When it was his turn, he bent his head in acknowledgment of the introduction and Lianon moved on to the next teacher. Simon did get a kick out of putting faces to the names Lola and Devlin had mentioned from the summer.

When the introductions were over, the Headmaster said they would meet with the department heads after breakfast. For the art department, it was one of the music teachers, a male fairy named Professor Barton.

It was a short meeting, held in Professor Barton's classroom. They reviewed the main rules of the Faculty Handbook which were fairly straightforward. Then they discussed possible themes for the end-of-term show and distributed various after-school activities among themselves.

Because Simon needed to return to Summerset every night for his recovery, he was not required to eat the evening meal at school. This had been explained briefly to the staff as being due to a medical condition.

Therefore, Simon chose to host activities on Saturday and Sunday mornings, an unpopular time slot. He planned to open his classroom to students wanting to work on personal creative projects or to advance classroom projects.

When the meeting ended, Simon went to his office to prepare and plan. The Academy did not offer a Visual Arts degree—the classes he would be teaching would be electives in Painting, Drawing, and Sculpture. Each subject had two levels. If a student had successfully completed all the classes, they could then enroll in a Mixed Media class. Students presented a project they wanted to work on during the semester, and their artistic productions were usually displayed on campus.

Not all seven classes were offered every semester. This semester, Simon would be teaching level one of all three subjects. These were morning classes held three times per week. He would have a small group for the Mixed Media class—these were afternoon classes, twice per week. It was a perfectly balanced schedule.

Simon had never been a professor. In fact, Simon had never had a job. He'd never questioned it; they were wealthy and he could do whatever he pleased. Which is exactly what he had done. He had painted, Traveled, attended seminars all over the world, visited every museum he could find, and read scores of books. He really had enjoyed his short life on Earth.

But in the last few years, he hadn't been enjoying it as much. He'd been living on borrowed time, searching for answers, expending energy, effort, and money needlessly. The solution had come to him. Another testament to having faith.

Perhaps he should start writing his memoirs, for the children of course. Or Devlin could include them in the Archives, as Simon hadn't realized at the time he was meant to be augmenting the book for future generations. Yes, that's exactly what he would do.

Every morning, with his cup of Morning Glory, he would dictate a part of his life story. It would be recorded in the Collective. When finished, he would request a written copy for the Knowledge Center.

He certainly wasn't going to write it by hand. Simon knew his strengths, and writing and rigor were not among them!

He took out the previous teacher's planner and syllabus. It was a bit dated. He made some changes to make the content more interesting and reflect his unique personality.

Each subject was divided into three equal parts: art history and appreciation, technique, and practical application. The previous teacher had solved this by allotting one hour per week to each part. He could do better, he thought.

He would split the one-hour lessons equally into three twenty-minute mini-lessons. He remembered how boring theoretical lessons could be when they dragged on. This way, the classes would feel more balanced and time would fly by.

Of course, that meant the students would only have twenty minutes for practical application. They were used to having a whole hour to paint, sculpt, or draw on Fridays. Simon felt this was still the better way, based on the knowledge he had absorbed. The classes were meant for instruction. If the students wanted time to express themselves creatively, they could join him on Saturday and Sunday mornings.

Taking the first lesson, he left his office and went to stand in front of the classroom.

"Welcome to Level 1 Drawing. My name is Professor Somin and it is an honor to have the opportunity to share my knowledge and experience with all of you. Please introduce yourselves by name, but also include your level of interest and proficiency in drawing," he said to the empty room.

He smiled to himself. *This is going to be fun.*

CHAPTER 40

DEVLIN

THE LAST FEW days before school started were busier than anticipated. Devlin was now Custodian and still learning how to manage the Estate. Of course, while he and Jackson would be away at school, the tasks would revert back to Phyllis.

He would be in college for the next four years. He didn't want Phyllis tethered to home because of him. He had delegated a few tasks to John before leaving for Summerset, and that had worked out well. Some tasks were automated with the help of technology. On Saturday morning, he decided to meditate to find ways to make the Estate manage itself.

That's when he remembered Alderan. Surely the High Elf could take on a more active role, considering his sole job was handling the Evers' affairs? Devlin gave him a call before breakfast and asked if he could come to the house for a meeting.

Alderan was, of course, available. While his integration was getting smoother, he had not yet started to interact socially.

"Be advised that I cannot offer legal counsel," he warned.

"I understand. I require management assistance," explained Devlin.

Alderan agreed and told Devlin he would be there at ten a.m. and they hung up.

At breakfast, Devlin told Phyllis and Lola to expect a visitor. Phyllis explained she and Lola were going shopping in Williamsburg and would likely have lunch in town as well.

"I'm sorry I'll miss him. I wonder what he looks like as a human," mused Lola.

"I had not thought of that!" exclaimed Devlin.

"Well, I'm sure we'll have ample opportunities to meet him in the coming years," replied Phyllis. "Meanwhile, we'll be having guests for dinner."

"Guests!?" cried Lola. Then lowering her voice she said, "Since when do you spring guests on us at the last minute, and on a day that's already busy?"

"I apologize, darling. I should have specified. Jackson came home late last night. He's resting now but will join us for drinks and dinner. I've also invited Boris," she explained.

"Oh! They're not guests, they're family!" exclaimed Lola, relaxing back into her seat.

"How much of our time in Summerset should we share with them?" asked Devlin.

"That is a tricky question. There were no warnings about sharing our experience there, and since Boris is a Traveler, he is aware of High Elves and their land, though I doubt he has visited. I haven't really discussed it with him. We've had other matters to attend to," replied Phyllis.

"Right, and Jackson knows that we went there and why we went there. It would be odd not to share the outcome with him. He must have been worried," said Lola.

"Not at all. I had Edward contact him to let him know all was well," said Devlin.

"Well done, Devlin. I admit I was rather focused on the task at hand, as it were," replied Phyllis.

"I am still adjusting to my role as Custodian and Head of the family. It is my duty to see to the welfare of this family, but I may differ from you and Father on some matters as I am still young and inexperienced," he said.

"How very mature of you, sugar," replied Phyllis, patting his hand. "I'm glad you reached out to Alderan for help. I admit I've gotten used to having Jackson and now you take over our financials. The work is much too serious for my bohemian personality."

"I like this Lord-of-the-Manor look on you. You should get a double-breasted blazer and an ascot," teased Lola.

"I do not think that will be necessary. We already have a jacket to wear at school. It is funny. I never dreamed of a life like this one when I was young," he said, wistfully.

"What did you want to do when you were a kid?" asked Lola.

"I wanted to be a mountain guide," replied Devlin.

"A mountain guide?!" exclaimed Phyllis. "You must get that from your mother's side. Evers tend to be sedentary intellectuals. No wonder you wanted to Travel to outdoor spots when I asked about vacation spots."

"Yes. My grandfather was a mountain guide. He died when I was twelve. Before he passed, he would take me hiking and camping as often as he could. He said a man needed to know how to survive in the wild and weather the elements," replied Devlin.

"So if we got stuck in the middle of nowhere, you could make sure we got out safely?" asked Lola.

"Yes, I believe that I could," replied Devlin, proudly.

"That is good to know," said Lola. "And we definitely chose the right man for the Custodian job!"

They finished up their breakfast while chatting about their respective childhoods. Devlin had missed out on family dinners growing up and he loved these impromptu, relaxed chats.

Not only was he getting to know his new family, but it deepened the bond between them.

CHAPTER 41

LOLA

"SO YOU THINK I should get back together with Tom?" asked Lola, taking a sip of iced tea.

They were having lunch at her favorite restaurant on the waterfront. Lola had ordered a lobster roll, and it was served with French fries, coleslaw, and corn on the cob. The corn was amazing at this time of year.

"Lola, you're only sixteen. It's not like you'll be marrying the boy anytime soon, or ever. Or have you left out important details?" asked Phyllis.

"No! We're just dating," replied Lola, alternately dipping her fries in ketchup, then mayo. They were crispy and salty, just the way she liked them.

"Well, there you go. Listen to what he has to say. Face to face, not texting. And see how you feel when you hear it. But listen with an open mind," suggested Phyllis. "The High Elves cleared him of any wrongdoing, but you must decide what you want from this relationship."

"That's good advice. It's what Sara suggested as well," replied Lola.

"Yes, I should take my own advice," muttered Phyllis.

"What was that?" asked Lola, raising her head from the last of her fries.

"Nothing, darling," said Phyllis, smiling at her niece. "Are you excited to go back to school tomorrow?"

"Yes, and no. On the one hand, I can't wait to see my friends and see what classes I'll have. On the other, I can't help but feel the last few months have been a whirlwind and I just haven't had time to settle. To just *be*," said Lola.

"I know what you mean!" emphasized Phyllis.

"I mean, most of what's happened is great. But I wish we'd had more time to enjoy each other as a family," she said.

"I agree, Lola. But you know, most kids your age are going off to college. It's a time in your life to explore new ideas, new people, and new places. It's a very exciting time! Even more so if you factor in our family's unique abilities," countered Phyllis.

"I know. I guess I'm just not as comfortable with change as Devlin is. He seems to be embracing his whole new life with gusto," said Lola with a laugh.

"Don't be so sure, darling. I think Devlin may have his own inse-cure moments. Don't forget to make time to spend with your brother. He's going to need you," replied Phyllis.

"He looks so sure of himself," said Lola, doubtfully.

"That's because men have been taught to be strong, capable, and provide. Devlin is still only a boy. Going back to school will do him good, especially as your father will be on hand," she said.

"That's definitely a positive thing about going back to school. I know he won't look like my dad, and we won't be able to call him that, but we get to see him home every day. I guess we're trading one parent for the other," said Lola.

Phyllis started to cry. Lola was horrified. She reached into her purse and gave her aunt a tissue.

"I'm so sorry, Phyllis, I didn't mean to hurt your feelings," she said in a panic, looking over her shoulder, worried they were attracting too much attention. But the other diners didn't seem to notice. Phyllis wasn't bawling her eyes out or anything, she was crying rather daintily and dabbing the tissue at her eyes.

"You didn't hurt my feelings, darling. You called me a parent," said Phyllis, her voice tremulous. She reached across the table and grabbed Lola's hand. "I know you loved your mother and no one could ever take her place. But you have no idea how happy it makes me feel that you consider me one of your parents because I consider you to be the daughter I never thought I could hope for."

Lola blushed and squeezed her aunt's hand. Then releasing it, she got up to hug her aunt.

"I love you, Phyllis. And I can't imagine my life without you. I miss you when I'm at school. But we'll see each other every Sunday, right?" said Lola, returning to her seat.

Phyllis nodded while blowing her nose. She did it discreetly, and rather lady-like. A task Lola had yet to master. When she blew her nose, it was like someone had pulled an elephant's tail.

"I love you too, Lola. And yes, I'll be there every Sunday, just you try to stop me," she said with a small hiccup.

CHAPTER 42

PHYLLIS

PHYLLIS DECIDED to take her own advice and bite the bullet. She made plans with Boris for the afternoon, saying she preferred to go somewhere where they could be alone and uninterrupted.

Boris assumed she wanted him to herself for an intimate night. She did not correct his assumption. First, because it served her purpose to have a private chat with him. And second, because her appetite for food was not the only one that had suddenly increased.

She asked her physician about it. Didn't most mothers have morning sickness in the first few months? He had assured her only a select few were afflicted and that everything was okay.

Boris took the news rather well. At first, she thought he'd gone into shock. Or hadn't heard her. She'd been so nervous, she simply blurted it out. Completely disregarding the tactful lead-in she had practiced in the tub at home.

"We'll be married at once," he eventually replied.

"We can discuss practicalities later, Boris. Tell me how you feel about this, first," she said.

He looked at her with confusion. "I am overjoyed, of course."

"You don't look overjoyed," she'd said, skeptically.

He looked at her then. Intently. Eyes boring into hers with such intensity that Phyllis started to squirm. He rose, walked to her, and took her hands, pulling her up from the bed where she sat.

"Phyllis Evers, I have loved you from the first moment I laid eyes on you. You are the most accomplished, graceful, and beautiful woman I have ever had the privilege to meet. I felt honored to be able to spend a week with you every year. Then when we found out we were both Travelers and could be together, I did not think I could ever be happier. But now you tell me you are carrying my child. The only possible way to top my joy right now is if you did me the honor of becoming my wife," exclaimed Boris, bending down on one knee for the last sentence.

He let go of one of her hands, reached into his pocket, and produced a small box. Relinquishing her other hand, he opened the box and Phyllis gasped.

"You see I had planned to ask you to marry me today. If you accept, it will be the happiest day of my life."

Phyllis looked at the box. It held an antique silver-colored ring which must have been in his family for generations. The band was studded with small diamonds and it was topped with an infinity symbol, also studded with small diamonds.

Taking her eyes away from the ring, she looked at Boris. He beamed at her.

"Yes! Of course, I'll marry you. Now get up before you hurt your knees," she said, laughing.

Before he got up, he took the ring from the box and slipped it onto her finger. Then he threw the box over his shoulder and rose to kiss her.

Now they were all seated at the dinner table, taking a breath before dessert. Phyllis had asked Sally to stay to serve the meal, as she did when they had guests. Before dinner, over drinks, Jackson had regaled them with tales from his trip, commenting on endless pictures. Before Sally left with the dinner dishes, she placed a cake and coffee on the sideboard. John came out with a bottle of sparkling apple juice, some flutes, and a bucket of ice.

"Are you celebrating our departure?" joked Devlin.

"No, Sugar, Boris and I have an announcement to make," she said as John poured the apple juice, brought them each a glass, and placed the bottle in the bucket. Phyllis thanked him and let him know that he and Sally were free to go. He gave a short bow and wished them *Bon appétit.*

Phyllis rose and everyone followed suit.

"Actually, we have two announcements to make. I wish Simon were here, but I'll tell him tomorrow," said Phyllis.

"This afternoon, your aunt Phyllis accepted my proposal of marriage," said Boris.

Lola clapped and Jackson hooted. Devlin beamed.

"What wonderful news! May you find joy and comfort in each other," he said, toasting the newly engaged couple.

They clinked glasses and everyone rose to hug and congratulate each of them.

"There's more," said Phyllis. "I'm pregnant. We should welcome a new member of the family in early May."

Everyone started talking at once. There was another round of congratulations.

"When's the wedding? Where will you live?" asked Lola, excited.

Everyone laughed and settled back down to enjoy their apple juice. It wasn't as good as champagne but Phyllis was happy to give it up for the time being.

"We haven't decided where we're going to live yet. As Boris is Custodian for his family, his permanent residence has to be the family home. I'm sure we'll figure something out," said Phyllis.

"As to the wedding," added Boris. "Your aunt wanted everyone to be present, so we decided to have it over the Holidays. The date has not yet been set."

"Fortunately, I shouldn't be showing too much by then. If I keep eating the way I have, Madame Beaufort will have her work cut out for her," exclaimed Phyllis.

"So that is why you have been eating with such an appetite. I thought it was because of Summerset," said Devlin. "Though my own appetite reverted back to normal after a day or two."

They had cake and coffee and talked about the upcoming plans to be made.

"Lola, would you be Maid of Honor?" asked Phyllis.

"I would love to. Thank you!" she exclaimed. "But I won't be around to help you out," she added, disappointed.

"Nonsense! We can have wedding planning meetings every Sunday. I will hire someone to help with the organization of it all," Phyllis said.

It was settled. Jackson thanked Phyllis for dinner and said he needed to stretch his legs. Devlin offered to accompany him and they left together.

Boris yawned and said he would say good night, as it was nearly two a.m. for him. He kissed Lola on the cheek and asked her to say hello to her father. He gave Phyllis a quick kiss and told her to call him in the morning.

Lola and Phyllis brought the dessert dishes and glasses into the kitchen for Sally to deal with in the morning. Instead of adjourning to the Library, they decided to go sit on the porch and talk about wedding themes and baby names.

CHAPTER 43
SIMON

AFTER ORIENTATION, Phyllis, Lola, and Devlin met with Simon in his office.

"Nice digs, Professor Somin," said Lola with a whistle.

"Thank you, Lola. I'm very comfortable here," he replied, inviting them to sit in front of the fire. It was much cooler at the Academy than it was in the South. Not cold enough to warrant lighting a fire, but there was one in the hearth all the same. Simon had been impressed by the magical option to have an actual wood fire, crackles and all, without the heat.

"So how are you settling in?" asked Phyllis.

"Wonderfully. Everyone has been very welcoming. Lola, you were right, the food is divine. However, I'll have to take your word for it about the coffee. It does not taste right to a High Elf. Most of the processed food doesn't sit well with our constitution," he explained.

"Bummer," said Lola.

"Have either of you registered for one of my classes?" asked Simon.

Lola shook her head no and added, "Sorry, Dad. I'm really not an artist."

Turning an expectant gaze to Devlin, he was rewarded with a smile.

"I have registered for Level 1 Drawing," said Devlin proudly.

Simon gave his shoulder a squeeze.

"How about you guys? Was it a great adjustment going back to your human lives?" he asked.

They each gave him a summary of what had been going on since they had seen him.

"I have some news, Simon. Good news," said Phyllis finally.

When he heard his sister was not only getting married but also having a baby, Simon leaped up, scooped up his sister, and spun her around in glee.

"Dad, be careful," said Lola, concerned.

"Right, sorry. I forgot I was taller and stronger. Are you okay, Phyllis?" he asked, still smiling at his little sister.

"I'm fine, Simon. Wonderful, in fact. We'll have the wedding over the Holidays so you can all attend. The baby won't be due until May. You'll get to meet him or her when you come home for the summer break," she explained.

"That's fantastic. I can't wait!" said Simon.

There was a tea tray on the coffee table and he asked them if they wanted any. When they declined, he added, "It's Morning Glory!"

They all had fond memories of the tea and decided this would be a Sunday afternoon ritual from now on.

"Any cookies?" asked Lola.

"I'm afraid not," replied Simon. "But I'll make sure I have some for next time."

They had tea and chatted about the upcoming semester and wedding plans until it was time for Phyllis to go home, and the kids to get to their dorm rooms.

CHAPTER 44
DEVLIN

DEVLIN WAS FINALLY GOING to be able to use the Sphere. On Tuesday and Thursday mornings, he had a one-hour class called World Jumping. He had expected it to be with Headmaster Lianon, but the name on his Schedule was Elder Lawrence.

Heading down the corridor near the Traveling classroom, Devlin found the room number he was looking for. It was one of the frosted doors they hadn't been able to access during the Summer Program.

He tried the handle, but it was locked. Checking his watch, he saw he was only five minutes early. The Professor had to be present. Devlin knocked and waited. Soon he was joined by another student. The girl introduced herself as Anita. Devlin introduced himself and told her the door was locked and that he had tried knocking. The girl thought for a moment, then tried her Key in the lock. It worked!

The door opened into what looked like a meeting room. Two other students, a girl and a boy, were seated at the table. Devlin and Anita sat down and introduced themselves to the others.

As the bell rang, a door appeared, and out came Elder Lawrence. Despite his title, he was not old. He looked like he was in his early forties. He was dressed like a hipster and carried a messenger bag like he'd just arrived on his bike instead of through a Traveling door.

"Good morning, everyone! I'm Elder Lawrence, but you may call me Lawrence."

He asked for their names and went around the room to shake their hands individually, saying *Nice to meet* you to each of them. He took a seat at the head of the table, opened his messenger bag, and produced four soft-covered textbooks which he slid across the table to each of them.

Devlin caught his textbook and read the title: *World Jumping 101: An Idiot's Guide to Exploring Other Worlds, by Lawrence Patterson.* He was not the only one to laugh. The other students were flipping through the pages of the textbook, trying to figure out if this was a joke.

"As you can imagine, this book was not published by the Academy, nor by any other respected publisher," he said, and one of the girls giggled. "However, it is the only curriculum available at present on the topic. The workbook was tested with last year's cohort of two students and has been updated to reflect their feedback. Your participation will likely yield an improved edition."

He asked them to turn to the Table of Contents where he outlined what they would be covering in this class, and what would remain for the winter semester class.

"For the first few weeks, we'll be covering the history, ethics, and mechanics of World Jumping. In November, we'll study the known worlds and what has been learned so far. In December, we will visit a few of the safer ones and discuss the benefits of regular interaction with these worlds," he explained.

"The workbook is mostly blank when I flip to the content for the winter term," stated Anita.

Devlin and the others flipped to the second part of the workbook. Indeed, there were a number of blank pages.

"Due to recent events, World Jumping is now banned," he said.

Students gasped and protested in confusion. Lawrence put up a hand to silence their objections.

"World Jumping for entertainment was never allowed. If you turn to page fourteen, you'll find out why the Council of Magical Earthly

Beings gave the Spheres to the first Elders. The purpose was to explore and gain knowledge, in the same way as Astronauts explore the Moon, other planets, and, eventually, other galaxies.

"In addition, the first Elders were wise, experienced Travelers. Humans with integrity who could be trusted to use the Sphere to learn from other worlds and record their findings in the Archives. In the same way they don't let just anyone go up into space; it takes years of diligent studies and training to even be considered for the space program.

"However, the Spheres were passed down from Elder to Elder without proper training. Custodians became Elders by default, not through rigorous screening and testing.

"But now that is about to change. Reform is upon us. The High Elves have seized all remaining Spheres. If you are still in possession of a family Sphere, it means you have been deemed worthy of instruction. Innocent until proven guilty, so to speak," he said and waited for their reactions.

"Who, aside from us, and presumably yourself, still has the use of their Spheres?" asked Lily.

"A new High Elder Council has been established. It will be composed of true Elders, those that have been selected by the Traveler Community for their integrity and contribution. My mentor, High Elder Whittaker, has an active Sphere. Since he has no living descendants, and I have no living ancestors, he has been training me for the last ten years. I will take his place on the High Elder Council when he dies.

"I have been tasked with training the next generation of World Jumpers. Last year, two students registered for this class. Over the summer, they were given two options: 1–Join a special task force to explore and record life on New Worlds, or 2–Relinquish their Sphere and forfeit World Jumping.

"You are lucky. I am going to give you the chance to choose between those two options now. If you choose option 2, you may leave and choose another elective. If you choose to stay, you will be given the opportunity to choose again at the end of this term, and at the end of the winter term. I believe it is a win-win situation," he said, and rose to let them discuss this among themselves.

"Just to be clear. We can take the full course, over two terms, and still walk away?" asked Oliver.

"Correct. If you complete the classes successfully, you will receive credits just like you would for any other elective," replied the Professor.

Lily thanked the professor and left the room. When no one else rose, he resumed his lecture.

CHAPTER 45
LOLA

WHILE DEVLIN WAS in World Jumping class, Lola was registered for Time Traveling, which was held in the regular Traveling classroom. Lola was disappointed not to have Lady Samsara as a teacher, but the actual teacher, Professor Ballantyne, was very cool.

The closest comparison Lola had to describe her was Amelia Earhart. She was wearing some kind of Steampunk outfit made of brown leather and beige linen. Instead of pants, she was rocking an Academy-approved knee-length skirt and long leather boots. Her blonde hair was coiffed in an unruly pixie cut and she wore neither makeup nor jewelry. She didn't look old enough to be a teacher.

There were eight students; the teacher had them introduce themselves and tell the class why they wanted to Time Travel. Lola knew this had to be a trick question. No one would dare answer that it was because it was beyond cool. She hoped she wouldn't be called on first so she would have time to formulate an appropriate response.

Unfortunately, Evers was the first name on the list.

"You must be Simon's daughter," Professor Ballantyne said.

Lola was caught off guard. This was an easy fact to check, but Lola didn't know if there would be follow-up questions regarding her dad's death or his new life as a High Elf. *Do the faculty know who Dad is?*

Lola went for a simple, "Yes, ma'am."

"I'm the one who taught him how to use the Time Watch," she explained. "Why do you want to Time Travel, Lola?"

Lola was still in her head about the thing with her dad and hadn't had time to come up with a reply, let alone a good one, and she blurted out, "Because I can."

Everyone laughed, but Professor Ballantyne narrowed her eyes at her. *Oh God*, thought Lola, *now she's going to think I'm some kind of delinquent*. She was about to explain herself, but the teacher shook her head and moved on to the next student. She had a great answer, which made Lola feel worse.

"To better understand the events that have shaped my nation," she said.

There were similar answers for the other students. When Professor Ballantyne heard from everyone, she distributed their textbooks and asked them to take out their notebooks. She explained about the reform on the use of magical Traveling Artifacts. Time Travelers were now required to submit their Traveling plans in advance to their local Council of Elders, much like a flight plan. This was to ensure the safety of Time Travelers and avoid any misuse of Time Watches.

Though Time Travelers had been receiving mandatory instruction at the Academy for decades, it seemed a group of ill-intentioned Travelers had used their watches to attempt to change events of the past and had somehow managed to wreak havoc on the time-space continuum. This was not meant to be possible. Their Watches had been revoked, and an independent team of investigators was currently interviewing all families with Time Watches to ensure compliance with the new rules.

Professor Ballantyne gave them each a copy of the syllabus. Lola was surprised to see a large portion of the content centered around physics. They would also be studying ethics, psychology, and philosophy.

"As you can see, we won't begin to study the Watch, let alone how to use it before the end of this term. You may now take a moment to decide whether or not you wish to continue with the class or choose another elective. Bear in mind that level 1 Time Travel is only offered in the Fall Term. If you choose to leave now and change your mind, you will need to wait a year to take it again," said the Professor.

Some of the girls discussed the matter among themselves. As Lola didn't know anyone, she read over the syllabus by herself and decided the coursework would not be difficult and the class would be worth it.

Three girls got up, thanked the teacher, and left the room.

"Time Travel used to be thought of as just science fiction, but Einstein's general theory of relativity allows for the possibility that we could warp space-time so much that you could go off in a rocket and return before you set out," she said after the door had closed. "Does anyone know who said that?"

One of the boys raised his hand. The teacher nodded at him and he said, "Stephen Hawking."

"That's correct. Turn to page eleven," she replied and the class began.

Lola was happy that she and Tom shared most of their classes. After her talk with Phyllis, Lola had texted Tom and requested they meet. He had offered to come to her house and she had accepted.

They'd gone to sit under the gazebo. Tom enjoyed the southern heat. Lola told him she would hear him out and tell him how she felt after he had finished. He had looked relieved to have an opportunity to explain. In the end, Lola realized he had been used by his mom and uncle and it wasn't his fault at all. They hugged, kissed, and all was right with the world.

She'd asked if he wanted to get his swimsuit and they could hang out by the pool.

"That would be great, but I've made plans with Keith and Lenora," he said.

"Right, they're still dating! What did you plan to do?" asked Lola.

"Nothing special, just hang out at my place," he replied.

"In that case, why don't you ask them to tag along? In fact, why don't I invite the whole gang?" said Lola.

"Are you sure about that? Don't you need to ask your aunt?" he suggested.

"Nah! She's cool. And besides, the pool is all the way over there, so we won't disturb anyone. So long as everyone knows it's just a pool hangout, not a booze party or anything," warned Lola.

"Not a problem. Since most of us are in dreary weather countries, this will be a treat. Of course, some of us might get in trouble for coming home past curfew, but that's not your problem!"

Lola sent the message while Tom went home to get his things. He came back faster than Lola thought possible. She walked him to the pool and told him she had to get her own swimsuit. She showed him the poolhouse where people could change if they arrived before she did.

On the way to the house, she saw most of her friends were texting that they were stoked and on their way. Devlin sent a single eyeglass emoji. Lola laughed and assumed that meant he was coming to make sure everyone behaved.

Lola went to her room to change and decided to take a page out of Devlin's book. She Traveled her way back to the pool. Traveling was so cool. When she arrived, she saw most of her guests were there and they had brought snacks: chips, soda, and candy!

"You guys are the best," she said, grabbing a licorice twist.

There were hugs and high-fives. Some of them had met over the break, but for most of them, it was the first time they got together since the Summer Program had ended. Which was barely two weeks ago, but that was ages in my teen years.

Colin found an audio system in the poolhouse and plugged his phone in to stream music and the party was off to a great start.

At one point, a door appeared and Keith's mom popped out to let him know it was time to come home. Keith was understandably mortified, and most of them tried really hard not to laugh. He barely had time to kiss Lenora before his mom grabbed him by the collar and dragged him through the door.

Everyone was in stitches after they left, but people started leaving. It was late in the UK and, curfew or not, they were tired. They were nice enough to help Lola and Devlin clean up before they left. It had been a great party.

Lola smiled as she remembered the party. They'd had a great time, and Lola had gotten to know Keith since he was in most of their classes.

After her first day back at school, Lola understood how they would be able to complete their last year of high school in a single semester: more cramming. But Tom was a good student and he would be her study buddy this time. He was a good friend and an even better boyfriend. He literally offered to carry her books when they went to class. Of course, she refused most of the time, but once in a while she played the maiden and let him. On those occasions, his chest would puff out like he'd just saved her from a lion. But hey, if it made him happy...

Now Lola sat in the common room looking around at her friends. Sara, ever the enthusiastic cheerleader. James, clever and thoughtful. Colin, master of shenanigans. Lenora, cutting wit with a heart of gold. Clara, the fairy princess. Devlin, everyone's big brother. Tom, the boy next door, and now Keith, the class clown.

Not four months ago, she had spent her evenings reading in her room. Most of her lunches at school had been spent the same way, tucked away near the chess club because that's where she would get the most peace and quiet.

She'd never realized how lonely she'd been. How much she wanted to fit in, to have friends, to be accepted. She looked at Devlin. He was laughing with the other boys, analyzing their last W&W game. He'd been alone too. Now they were a family.

Lenora and Clara were working the room, looking for people to join the social committee and their crusade to extend the curfew.

And right next to Lola was Sara, staring at Devlin in open admiration. Lola nudged her friend and said, "Want to go back to the room and talk about boys?"

Sara laughed. "You just want to eat some of my candy," she replied.

"You know me so well," said Lola.

They got up, arm-in-arm, and said good night to their friends. It was going to be a great school year.

EPILOGUE

, December 26, 2020

It was the social event of the year. Unfortunately, it was somewhat an exclusive affair, as Boris and Phyllis' wedding at the Williamsburgh Inn had been contained to one hundred and fifty guests.

At first, Phyllis had wanted to have it at the house, as they could accommodate more guests. But Boris did not want her overexerting herself, not only because of the baby but because it was her wedding and she should enjoy every minute of it. Also, since many guests would be flying in from all over the world, choosing a hotel as a wedding venue had seemed like a better option. In the end, Phyllis had hired their wedding coordinator, Felicia, and let the woman do all the heavy lifting.

She would take the wedding binder to Lola on Sunday afternoons, and they would choose from the items Felicia had short-listed. It has been an effortless and thoroughly enjoyable process.

As Lola walked down the aisle in her lilac maid-of-honor dress, she smiled at the guests. She would be meeting Boris's family for the first time during the reception. But on the Evers side, she saw familiar faces like Bonnie and Jackson, Edward Jr. and his family, Alderan, Phyllis' friends from town, and their new friends, in human form, from Summerset. Tom, her date for the evening, winked at her. He looked so handsome in his tuxedo. Everyone looked amazing.

When she arrived at the altar, which was a wisteria-covered arch, Lola smiled at Boris. He looked so dashing in his pale gray suit and lilac bow tie. Beside him stood his son and best man, Aleksei. Aleksei was married to Galeena, seated in the first row with baby Anton on her lap. Their daughter, Anoushka, aka the flower girl, had preceded Lola down the aisle with a basket of purple rose petals.

The assembly turned at the sound of an approaching carriage. The coach steadied the horses and opened the carriage door.

Devlin offered a hand to Phyllis and helped her down the steps. The wedding march began, and everyone rose to watch them proceed down the aisle. Once he had delivered Phyllis to Boris, Devlin kissed her cheek and went to sit next to Aeriearie, his date for the evening. He and Sara were still getting to know one another. And since Aeriearie knew Phyllis while Sara had only met her in passing, she had seemed like a better choice.

Phyllis gave her bouquet to Lola and took Boris' hands as they faced the officiant. He was a tall man, wearing unusual silvery-gray robes, and sporting very long blond hair. Simon beamed at Boris and Phyllis and asked the assembly to be seated.

They had debated on how to include Simon in the ceremony while inviting non-Traveler guests. In the end, it was Alderan who had suggested Simon come as his *new* self. When visiting for less than a day, High Elves were not required to take human form. They could also conceal the Elvish appearance to blend in. Thus Simon did not have pointy ears and was shorter, though still taller than most guests. He looked every bit the part of a Druid, which most guests took in stride. A lot of people hired cosplay wedding officiants now for non-denominational ceremonies.

Because it was the day after Christmas, they had opted for a festive theme of silver and purple. They had kept the Christmas trees and other decorations, only changing those that did not fit with the color scheme. The result was truly magical as if the whole day was tinsel-touched.

Though the ceremony and cocktails had been outdoors, the reception was indoors. While the wedding party was busy with pictures, guests roamed the beautifully manicured gardens, sipping champagne and eating hors d'oeuvres.

Felicia arranged the reception line, cued the music, and the guests cheered the newlyweds as they entered the reception hall for the five-course wedding feast. Lola and Devlin were seated at the main table for dinner, with Boris and Phyllis and Aleksei and his wife. They had hired a nanny to care for the children, and they were safely settled in their room for the evening.

Tom, Aeriearie, Bonnie, and Jackson were seated with Matthew and Sheila Maxwell and Boris' daughter Marina and her fiancé. It had been a good mix, and they seemed to be enjoying each other.

When it was time for toasts, Lola took out her note cards from her purse. They had agreed Aleksei would go first. Lola took deep breaths while keeping her face neutral and listening to the best man's speech. When it was her turn, she walked to the microphone.

"Good evening, everyone. I hope you are all having fun," she started and heard her friends cheering her on. She also heard Devlin in her mind, telling her she could do this. He knew she was nervous.

"I'd like to thank Felicia for making this an event to remember as well as those guests who came from far away and who are likely very tired due to the time difference. Thank you all for making the journey.

"As most of you know, I am Phyllis's niece. I only met her last June when my mother died. Not only did Phyllis open her home to me, but she opened her heart. She has become a second mother to me, and I don't know where I'd be without her.

"The first time I met Boris, he helped us out of a tricky situation, no questions asked. His priority was to make sure Phyllis and anyone connected to her were safe and secure. I will always remember him as dependable, loyal, and, if I may be allowed an antiquated term: debonair."

There was a rustle of laughter from the assembly.

"Every time I see Phyllis and Boris together, I see the way they look at each other. They are not as lovesick or infatuated, but as true friends, soul partners, and a marital bliss model. I hope I can find someone to experience that with one day.

"A great poet once wrote the most amazing lines about love:

"You know you're in love when you can't fall asleep because the reality is finally better than your dreams. Dr. Seuss.

"Let's all raise our glasses to the bride and groom and wish them a lifetime of love and joy!"

Lola raised her glass, and everyone got up.

"To the bride and groom!" she said, and there was an echo across the room. Despite requests against it, people started tapping their wine glasses for a kiss. Boris and Phyllis laughed and indulged them with a passionate kiss. There were hoots and catcalls.

Once the toasts were concluded, the games began. The purpose behind the games was to let the wait staff remove the main course dishes and serve the next course.

Once dinner was over, the dancing started. Lola was thrilled to dance with her father, even if he looked like a High Elf. She danced with Tom, of course, and also with her brother and Jackson. She thought dancing with Jackson might be awkward but they were good enough friends it wasn't awkward at all. Tom teased that he was jealous and Lola swatted his arm.

She danced with Boris; he almost made her cry. "You know, Lola, you and I are family now. I know your father is nearby but think of me as you would a stepfather. I will always be here for you, and your well-being and happiness are among my top priorities."

She was so choked up, all she could do was hug him tightly and kiss his cheek.

Soon it was time to cut the cake and throw the bouquet. Around ten p.m., some of the older guests said good night and retired to their rooms or went home if they were locals.

By midnight, the bride and groom had called it a night, and only those under twenty were still on the dance floor. The band and DJ apologized and started packing up, lights were being switched off, and Lola was surprised she had stayed up this late.

She made sure no one had left any important personal effects at the Head Table. As she was walking over to where Devlin and Tom were slumped on armchairs, a waiter stopped to give her an envelope. It read *Lola*. Thinking the guys couldn't get into any more trouble, she walked out of the room and into the gardens to stand under a lamplight.

It was a letter, and the handwriting seemed familiar.

Dear Lola,

I wrote this letter and sent it to your aunt Phyllis in Virginia with instructions to wait until you were back on your feet before she gave it to you.

As I write these lines, you are studying for a science test, as usual. I know you're worried about me, but you're still giving school your all because you know how important good grades are to me. You've always been a trooper.

I know I've been hard on you, always expecting the best, pushing you to do better. And if it seemed like I wasn't proud of you, that could not be further from the truth. You have so much talent and raw potential I don't want to see you waste it. You're a good person and a hard worker. I know you'll go far in life. Hopefully, further than me.

I did my best to provide a safe and stable home. I would have loved for you to grow up with two parents. But even if your dad had lived, living with him would have been neither safe nor stable. Don't get me wrong, *your father was brilliant. He was funny, gorgeous, and very talented. But he had no goals, no life purpose. Lord knows I loved him, but it wasn't meant to be.*

I hope you find some measure of happiness with Phyllis. From what I remember, she was a bit of an airhead, but she loved her brother fiercely and I know she'll take good care of you.

I hope by now you've forgiven me for dying and uprooting your whole life.

I know how much you always loved Dr. Seuss, so I'll leave you with a quote:

"Don't cry because it's over. Smile because it happened."

Love,

Mom

Lola felt a hand on her shoulder and looked up. It was her dad. Seeing her tears, he asked her what was wrong. She gave him the letter, and he read it.

He smiled, he cried, and he laughed. Probably about that bit about Phyllis being an airhead. He folded the letter and gave it back to Lola. He extended his arm, and Lola took it.

"Do you mind if I tuck you into bed before I go?" he asked.

Lola smiled and walked out into the night with her father.

The End

If you enjoyed this book, please consider leaving a review on
Amazon, Goodreads, or Bookbub.
Reviews help me reach new readers.

Join my Newsletter for writing updates, sales and giveaways!

The story continues in **The Blood Mage**, the first book in the **Blood Magick Trilogy** from <u>Tom's</u> point of view!

Turn the page for a sneak peak!

SNEAK PEAK
THE BLOOD MAGE

Up until this moment, it had been an epic birthday party.

Initially, Tom hadn't even wanted a party. It had seemed too soon for happiness. But when Aidan McCarthy, his mother's brother, had moved in after dad died last April, their home had become a vibrant, happy place again. Aidan never did things by half measures and had decided the family had lived under a cloud of cancer and sadness for too long. Aidan had challenged Tom to live again, starting with a celebration of his sixteenth birthday no one would soon forget.

Tom had retorted by telling Aidan that if he wanted a party so bad, then he could be the one to prepare it.

That might have been a mistake.

Of course, Aidan did things in a big way. Tom's uncle was a proper big-shot film producer. He was a three-time Irish Film & Television Academy Award winner and two-time American Academy Award, nominee. He had achieved this success partly on his own merits and partly through magical strategic partnerships.

Not that any of this had mattered to Tom. While he already knew he had the best uncle a guy could ever have, it never even occurred to him just what Aiden's line of work would have to do with creating a birthday blowout, the likes of which his friends had never seen.

As it turned out, one of Aidan's key partners was the famous Illusionist Ivan Lazarus. Though Ivan was known the world over by the non-magical community as the next Houdini, he had an impressive client list in the magical community. Ivan could make anyone see anything. Even large groups. Suffice it to say that when Aidan told Tom he'd gotten Ivan to do his sixteenth birthday party, Tom had thanked him profusely, thinking only of how impressed his friends were going to be and how he might use this particular stunt to maybe show off a little for his girlfriend, Lola. Not that he needed to impress her. It just felt good to be able to.

It never occurred to Tom to ask questions. Later, much later, he would realize just how stupid that had been. Right now, though, he wasn't thinking about the party at all except in passing, wondering that the catering staff had been able to erase all traces of their 1920s Speakeasy, which had been the theme of the murder mystery event.

He paused to smile, thinking about the enormous tent erected. The moment you'd stepped inside, you could have sworn you had been transported back in time to an underground club from the 1920s. What had surprised him was just how much the guests had thrown themselves into the themes. They could have just worn costumes, but Aidan had to take things to the next level. He'd written roles and scripts for all twenty guests; Josephine Baker, Charlie Chaplin, F. Scott Fitzgerald, Coco Chanel, and other great names of the era. All guests, in full costume, attended a lavish dinner party first, where they had to interact in character. There were signature cocktails like Sidecars and Gin Rickeys. All that and a great live jazz band to round out the evening.

When the guests had solved the murder, the club disappeared, and the staff and entertainers went home. All but the DJ who stayed for as long as the guests wanted to dance and party. The evening had been a night to remember, only ending when people had become too tired to dance. Eventually, though, the crowd had thinned out. With most of the guests staying in the guest bunkrooms, it had gotten quite late when they'd called it a night. There'd been much laughter and the goal of sleeping as late as they liked, though there was a brunch planned the next day.

Well, all except for Tabitha.

While Tom's sister had been enthusiastic about the party and had been on for his strongest supporters, she drew her line at sleeping with the rest in the bunk rooms. She wasn't against socializing, but she preferred having her things around her and the comfort of her own bed, claiming the bunk room mattresses would wreak havoc with her beauty sleep. To that end, Tabitha had gone to bed early, separating herself from the crowd. In some ways, Tom wondered if she was a clever girl, to find a way to keep her freedom when the house was so packed.

Something he was starting to regret he hadn't done.

Intent on fully immersing himself in the celebration Tom had bunked with his friends. He had also set the alarm for five-thirty, hoping to join Lola, his girlfriend, in her morning meditation. Lola and Sara had gone to bed at midnight.

What an ungodly hour, thought Tom, quickly silencing his watch so he wouldn't wake the others, not that he'd needed it. He hadn't so much as shut his eyes, too busy thinking about all that had happened that night and how he hoped to continue his birthday celebration a little more privately this morning.

The things you do for love! A smile crept across his face. His head was aching. He and the guys had crawled into the bunks at around three a.m. and swiftly passed out, which was good. They were all still dead to the world, with not so much as the flicker of an eyelash to indicate any of them were aware he was up and moving around in his bunk, trying to figure out where he'd put his socks or if he should have maybe tried for a bit of sleep after all.

Sleep. Yeah. Like I'd have heard the alarm if I had. Tom yawned and told himself he hadn't minded staying up all night. He would never have fallen asleep with all that snoring anyway.

Gingerly, he climbed down the ladder as quietly as he could. But as he got to the floor, he realized Devlin, Lola's brother wasn't in his bed.

He mused that getting up early had to be a family thing and wondered how he had missed him leaving. More worrying was the idea Devlin and Lola might be meditating together. That was the whole point of the escapade, to spend time alone with Lola. To surprise her with a cup of coffee and a view of the Channel. He hadn't exactly wanted company for all that.

He grabbed his t-shirt, jeans, and shoes from the pile on the floor and crept out of the room. Heading to the kitchen, he tried to think if he had ever gotten up this early. It certainly was quiet, even with so many guests in the house. He made a pot of coffee and reluctantly prepared three travel cups in case he had to offer one to Devlin.

Placing the cups on a small tray, he went out through the patio doors and onto the deck. They weren't by the pool or on the lawn beyond it. He shrugged and headed down the path to the Channel. It was a beautiful morning, the sun was just rising out of the water to greet him, bathing the entire world in a soft, golden glow. But other than a lone fisherman, there was no one else to greet him.

Frowning, he stalked back towards the house. He abandoned his tray on a table in the foyer and tiptoed to the girls' bunkroom. Easing the door open, he popped his head into the room. Only three beds were occupied. No Lola. He closed the door gently and headed back to the boys' room wondering if he'd missed something. Devlin wasn't back.

Where are they? Had they left without telling him?

Confused and starting to get kind of mad that nothing was going as he'd hoped it would, Tom stopped and considered what to do. It was much too early to update his mother and uncle, and he was tired. If they had left, it was their own business. They weren't exactly little kids and certainly didn't need anyone's permission to go home if they wanted to.

It was rude, though. And more than a little hurtful. Lola especially should have said something.

Grumpy from lack of sleep and more than a little put out, Tom stripped down to his underwear, made his way to the top bunk, and lay down to think things over.

Instead, he promptly fell asleep, dismissing Lola entirely from his mind, something else he probably shouldn't have done.

Click here to keep reading!

www.ingramcontent.com/pod-product-compliance
Lightning Source LLC
Chambersburg PA
CBHW020329260626
47156CB00004B/1441